In my imagination, I was taking off on the biggest wave of the day. The other surfers pointed and stared enviously as I . . .

"Kate! Katie, are you in there?"

"Oh, gee! I'm sorry, I've just been a little preoccupied lately."

"No kidding," Chris said. "Your dad just told me you're definitely working for the Bensons this summer. Kate, I thought we'd agreed—"

"We didn't agree to anything," I interrupted. "You're the one who wants me to stay home this summer. It's my summer vacation and if I want to spend it at the shore, I will!"

Caprice Romances from Tempo Books

A CAPRICE ROMANCE

Surfer Girl

FRANCESS LIN LANTZ

TEMPO BOOKS, NEW YORK

SURFER GIRL

A Tempo Book / published by arrangement with
the author

PRINTING HISTORY
Tempo Original / November 1983

ISBN: 0-441-79101-8

Tempo Books are published by The Berkley Publishing Group,
200 Madison Avenue, New York, New York 10016.
Tempo Books are registered in the United States Patent Office.
PRINTED IN THE UNITED STATES OF AMERICA

Surfer Girl

Chapter One

As the huge blue wave swelled beneath me, I stretched out on my surfboard and started paddling as hard as I could. The wind blew my hair straight back and salt water sprayed in my eyes, but I kept going. When the wave began to curl I stood up, crouched forward and shot down the enormous wall of water. I could hear the crowd on the beach cheering as I hung ten, grabbed the rail and—

"Kate McGovern!"

I was so lost in my surfing fantasy that for a second I couldn't figure out who was calling my name. I must have looked pretty blank, because Chris nudged me and whispered, "Kate, go ahead."

In a flash, it all came back to me. I wasn't in Hawaii, surfing the Banzai Pipeline. I was in The Cowpoke Room of Jimmy's Steak House, where Fairbanks High School was holding its annual end-of-the-year sports banquet. Coach Mahoney stood behind the podium, clutching my junior varsity letter, and my boyfriend, Chris Trower, sat next to me. Across the table, my father was smiling

1

proudly while Mom whispered something in his ear.

Before anyone could notice I'd been daydreaming, I leaped up and headed for the podium. "Kate won a first place in the regional finals this year, and she was co-captain of the team," Coach Mahoney was saying.

When I reached the podium, the coach shook my hand and gave me my letter. Everyone applauded and I could see Chris and my parents grinning at each other. As I held the soft blue and white F, my surfing dreams were momentarily forgotten. I thought back over the school year to all the practices, all the long bus rides to swim meets at rival schools, all the victories and defeats. It had been a good year, and winning my letter was the perfect way to end it. I smiled proudly and hurried back to my seat as Coach Mahoney called the next athlete's name.

I put my letter on the table next to my empty coffee cup and half-eaten piece of lemon meringue pie and glanced at my parents. Mom was wearing one of those "how my little girl has grown" looks. Dad was smiling at me and running his thumb and index finger over his new mustache. He'd just grown it a week ago and he kept touching it, as if he couldn't believe it was really there.

Chris reached under the tablecloth and took my hand in his. Chris is a basketball player and he has very large hands. Tonight they were hot and sweaty, probably because Chris was pretty sure he was going to win the team's Most Valuable Player Award. My hand felt like it was trapped inside a hothouse.

Chris had been my boyfriend for almost two years. We'd met the first day of sophomore year, when Chris walked into the girls' locker room by mistake. That made him pretty unforgettable, so when we ended up next to each other in the lunch line, we just naturally started up a conversation. Before long we were dating, and by junior year no one could imagine Kate without Chris or Chris without Kate. We were practically inseparable.

But for some reason, Chris had been really bugging me lately. I didn't know why, really, since nothing about him had changed. He still quoted basketball statistics as he walked me to class, he still picked me up in his battered old Buick and took me to Marx Brothers' movies, and we still spent lots of time at Bowman's Cliff, dreaming about our future together and making out.

Something was different though, and I couldn't quite put my finger on it. I felt restless and bored and irritable, and everything about Chris annoyed me—the ancient gravy stain on his green paisley tie (he once told me his mom had bought it for his first communion), the tuft of wavy brown hair that always stuck up on the back of his head, even the freckle on his earlobe that I had once found so attractive. And in the past, I knew, his sweaty hands wouldn't have bothered me. I would have leaned over and whispered, "Don't worry, Chris. I love you even if you don't win the Most Valuable Player Award." Then I would have kissed the freckle on his ear. But tonight I just sat there, listening to Coach Mahoney and feeling the perspiration form between Chris's palm and mine. It was really depressing.

"And the Most Valuable Player Award for the Fairbanks High School basketball team goes to . . . Chris Trower."

Chris's hand slid moistly from mine and with a joyous grin on his face, he loped up to the podium to claim his award—a wooden trophy with a huge silver basketball on it. I applauded along with everyone else, but when the basketball coach started listing Chris's achievements, I tuned out. I already knew what a terrific forward Chris was, and besides, there was something more important I had to think about, something that had been monopolizing my thoughts ever since last night, when my parents had finally given their permission.

Surfing . . . summer vacation . . . Beach Haven, New Jersey. Even now, those seven words get me so excited I can barely function, so it's no wonder I was pretty distracted that night. You see, for as long as I can remember, my family has spent the last two weeks of August at the New Jersey shore. We always go to the same place—Beach Haven on Long Beach Island—and for the last three years we've even rented the same cottage, a little place on Liberty Avenue, just a block away from the beach.

My whole family loves the shore. It's kind of crazy, really, because except for my father, we all have fair hair, freckles, and skin that turns the color of a lobster after fifteen minutes in the sun. My brother John has it the worst. He's got strawberry blond hair and head-to-toe freckles. The summer before he went to college, he got a job as a lifeguard, but he had to quit after the first day. Even with sunglasses, suntan lotion and a broad-brimmed hat he almost came down with sunstroke. I'm a little bit luckier. I have red hair and a patch of freckles on my cheeks and shoulders, but as long as I bathe my body in suntan lotion, I can usually stay out for an hour or two before I begin to bake. My dad has it best—he's got brown hair and a year-round tan—so it's not surprising that he's the one who took up sailing and got my mother interested enough to agree to summers at the shore.

Anyway, vacations on Long Beach Island have always been a real joy for me, but last summer was undoubtedly the best. For years I'd seen the surfers riding up and down the Island with their boards on top of their cars, or paddling out to catch a few final waves before sunset. I'd seen them, but I never really noticed them—until last summer.

Maybe it was joining the swim team at school and being forced to do all those laps with a kickboard to build up my leg muscles. Or maybe it was just that it suddenly seemed all the really good-looking boys in Beach Haven were carrying surfboards. I don't know, but suddenly I was interested in surfing. And when I get interested in something, watch out!

I rented a board and went out every day, always to one of the least popular beaches so I wouldn't have to endure the stares and jokes of the real surfers, most of whom were male. At first, I couldn't even figure out how to get my board in the right position to catch a wave, let alone stand up and ride. But by the end of the second week, I was actually surfing—not very well, of course, but competently enough to realize I was hooked. Surfing is terrific!

Chris had brought his trophy back to the table, and the football coach was showing a film of the year's highlights, but I was miles away. I was thinking about this summer, when for the first time in my life, I would be spending my entire summer vacation at the shore. And it was all thanks to Bill and Tina Benson. I've been babysitting for them for two years—ever since their son Ricky was born—and both Ricky and his sister Dee really like me. The Bensons own a house in Beach Haven and this year they'd asked me to come along as a mother's helper. I could hardly believe it when my parents said okay. I was going to spend all summer at the beach. An entire two and a half months of surfing!

In my imagination, I was on Long Beach Island, taking off on the biggest wave of the day. I did a radical fin-out aerial and shot down the face. The other surfers pointed and stared as I—

"Kate! Kate? Yoo-hoo, Katie, are you in there?"

I looked up to find that everyone was leaving. The sports banquet was over and Chris and my father were already walking toward the door. Mom was putting on her sweater and staring at me.

''Sorry, Mom. I guess I was daydreaming.''

''I've noticed a lot of that lately,'' observed my mother. ''You know, I don't think Chris is very happy. You didn't even congratulate him on winning the Most Valuable Player Award.''

''Oh, gee, I'm sorry.'' Contritely, I grabbed my letter and ran to catch up with Chris. ''Chris,'' I said, as my dad moved away to join my mother, ''congratulations! Your trophy looks great.''

''Thanks,'' he said glumly. ''I didn't think you'd noticed.''

''Sure I did. I've just been a little preoccupied lately.''

''No kidding. Your dad just told me you're definitely working for the Bensons this summer. Kate, I thought we'd agreed—''

''We didn't agree to anything,'' I interrupted. ''You're the one who wants me to stay home this summer.''

''Well, why not?'' demanded Chris, pushing his brown curls out of his eyes. ''You're my girl and it's only right we should spend the summer together.''

My girl. *My girl*! That was the way Chris always referred to me, but up until a few months ago, it had never bothered me. I was proud of being Chris's girlfriend. I'd never wanted to be with anyone else. But lately, Chris didn't seem so much loving as possessive. It was as if I was something that belonged to him, something he owned, and I was starting to realize I didn't like being thought of that way.

''Listen, Mr. Most Valuable Player, I can do whatever I please. It's my summer vacation and if I want to spend it at the shore, I will!'' I was getting really worked up, but then I noticed how upset Chris looked. His brow was furrowed and his mouth seemed to be trembling a little. As we left the restaurant, I gazed up into his handsome gray eyes and said, "I really want to go surfing, Chris. Besides, you can always come visit me."

"I know, but not that much. You know I'm working for my dad this summer, and he's already got jobs lined up through July." Chris's father owns a successful house-painting business and naturally summer is his busiest season.

"Well, think of it this way," I suggested. "No matter how much I lie on the beach, your tan is still going to be better than mine."

Chris didn't laugh. The parking lot of Jimmy's Steak House was mostly empty and I noticed my parents were waiting inside our car. I guess they could see that Chris and I were having a serious conversation, because Dad didn't honk the horn the way he usually does when I'm late. Chris's parents were in Ohio at his aunt's funeral and Chris had driven over in his old gray Buick. Normally he would have wanted to drive me home, but tonight he didn't even offer.

"Well . . ." I began cheerfully.

"I guess you figure you'll meet some handsome surfer this summer," Chris said suddenly. I didn't answer. What could I say, when Chris had read my thoughts so accurately? When I wasn't dreaming about the great surfing I would do that summer, I was fantasizing about the tall, blond surfer boy I would meet. It would be love at first sight, of course, and he would . . .

"I'm asking you one last time," Chris told me. "You're my girl, Kate. Are you going to stay with me this summer?"

They say redheads have terrible tempers, and I guess I proved it that night. Maybe I'd heard Chris call me "his girl'' one too many times because something inside me suddenly snapped. "Stop calling me 'your girl'!" I screamed. "I'm going to the shore this summer and there's absolutely nothing you can do to stop me!"

Before Chris could answer, I ran to our car, jumped in the back seat and slammed the door. Both my parents turned around to look at me, but neither one said a word. As we drove out of the parking lot of Jimmy's Steak House, I saw Chris sitting in his Buick. He looked pretty miserable, but at that moment I didn't care. I couldn't wait for school to end so I could take off for the shore and leave Fairbanks High far behind. I didn't need Fairbanks and I certainly didn't need Chris Trower. Pretty soon I'd be at the shore, surfing and sunbathing and cruising up and down the island with some well-built, good-looking guy.

I leaned my head back against the seat and stared out the back window at the stars. "Long Beach Island, watch out," I whispered. "This is going to be the most fabulous summer of my entire life!"

Chapter Two

Despite our big argument outside Jimmy's Steak House, Chris and I didn't break up. We didn't actually make up either. The main reason was that we barely saw each other. There was only one more week of school and we both had finals. After that, Chris started working for his father and I spent all my time getting ready for my summer at the shore.

I planned to call Chris three or four times before I left but something always seemed to come up. I wanted to get together with my friends Rachel and Amy before I left and my parents wanted me to clean up my room and spend some time with them too. I also spent a lot of time shopping for the perfect bathing suit. (Suits, actually. I bought two since I figured I'd be wearing them constantly.) I finally decided on a skimpy black bikini for sunbathing and a turquoise and black striped tank suit for surfing. I was tempted to buy two bikinis, but surfing is a strenuous sport and I could just picture the top of my bathing suit falling off while I was out there paddling for a wave or something. I mean, I'd have to stay underwater just to keep from dying of embarrassment, and then I'd probably drown anyway!

I also bought new jeans, shorts, three tops, sunglasses, sandals, and six bottles of suntan oil. Mom had lent me her charge cards and something about the feel of all that plastic money in my hands made me go wild. I figured I was safe though. Dad wouldn't get the bill until I was gone and by the end of the summer I'd have enough money to pay him back if I had to.

Mom and Dad had big plans for the summer, so they didn't really mind that I was going away. My brother John was staying at college to take summer school courses and with me gone, this would be their first summer all alone for almost twenty years. They were planning lots of day trips and a couple of long weekends in the Poconos as well as their usual two weeks in Beach Haven at the end of August.

The Bensons were coming to pick me up on Monday afternoon. Ten minutes before they were supposed to show up, I was still jamming things into my parents' ancient brown suitcases. With both kids away this summer, there weren't going to be enough suitcases to go around, so Mom and Dad were going to buy themselves some new ones. I was happy with the old ones though. They smelled like leather, mothballs and after-shave and I liked to think they were veterans of lots of trips as exciting and special as I hoped this one would be.

The Bensons were late, as usual. There was something about having two little kids, they said, that always slowed them down. Bill and Tina tended to be a little disorganized in general, though, so I was used to them doing things like forgetting their house keys or showing up a half-hour late.

When I finally forced the suitcases shut and dragged them downstairs, my mom and dad were talking to Tina Benson in the living room. Tina is an artist. She designs note cards and stationery that're sold in lots of craft stores in Pennsylvania and New Jersey. She has short blond hair and tiny features, and even though she's over thirty, she usually just wears jeans and casual blouses. She looks really good in them too, not like our gym teacher, Ms. Lipsky, who tries to look young by perming her hair and wearing Calvin Klein jogging outfits. Even in designer clothes she still looks about eighty-five and really awful.

Bill is an artist, too. He works for a big commercial art firm in Philadelphia and I guess he's a pretty big deal there because they let him spend the whole summer at the shore and he just has to go into the office once in a while. Bill is a big teddy bear of a guy. He has wild black hair, a full beard and a huge, football player-type body. Whenever he laughs I always think of a department store Santa Claus, holding his stomach and saying, "Ho, ho, ho!"

Mom and Dad followed me to the car reciting the usual list of dos and don'ts. "Call us if you need anything. . . . Don't go out without telling Bill or Tina where you're going. . . . Do you want to take some vitamins? . . . Remember, while you're in their house, you must obey the rules Bill and Tina set up for you. . . ."

Fortunately, neither Mom nor Dad mentioned anything about surfing. They'd let me surf last summer, but I knew they thought it was dangerous. I think they figured it was just a fad I'd grow tired of so they decided not to make a fuss about it. Besides they know I'm a good swimmer. I don't know what they thought about the surfing magazines I'd been reading all winter, but if they weren't going to say anything, I sure wasn't. After I bought a surfboard I could write a letter and break it to them gently.

When Dee and Ricky saw me, they got excited. "We're going to the o-cean!" shouted Ricky. "The o-cean, the o-cean!" Ricky is a cute two-year-old with dark curly hair like his father. He'd just started talking in complete sentences and the only time he stopped was when he fell asleep.

"Katie, Katie!" cried Dee. "Sit in the back seat with me!"

I couldn't see that I had much choice. The back of the Bensons' sky blue station wagon was crammed full of suitcases, toys, lawn chairs and beach umbrellas. The front seat was taken up by Bill, a large cooler, a couple of thermoses and a pile of maps. The only available space was in the back seat next to Ricky's carseat, and even that was covered with picture books, toys and a box of Animal Crackers.

"Okay," I told Dee. "I'll sit between you and Ricky."

Dee grinned. She's a thoughtful six-year-old, much quieter than Ricky, with messy blond hair that bobs against her shoulders. It's easy to take care of her because she likes me a lot and unlike Ricky, she usually does anything I ask.

There was no more room in the back of the car, so Bill got out and tied my suitcases to the roof. He did a good job, but I was still a little worried they might fly off when we got on the highway. They were so heavy, they'd probably crush anything they fell on. I started to giggle, imagining the headline: TRACTOR TRAILER DESTROYED BY FLYING SUITCASES.

No one noticed me, despite my giggles. Dee and Ricky were loudly arguing over the crayons and Bill was back in the car, trying to quiet them. Tina was explaining something about my work schedule to my parents, but I couldn't hear her over the kids' voices. Actually, I was rather curious about that myself. Tina had outlined my hours when she first offered me the job, but I was so excited about spending a summer at the shore, I'd barely listened.

I walked over to my parents, but Tina was done talking. "I guess we're all set," she said, and got back in the car.

It was then that I realized I was actually leaving. I wasn't going to see my parents or our familiar red brick house until the end of August. I was going away to live with a family I only knew casually, in a house I'd never seen, without any kids my own age.

When my mother hugged me, I didn't want to let go. "I'm going to miss you," I whispered.

"Have a wonderful summer," she said. "We'll miss you too. We love you."

Then it was Dad's turn, and the smell of his after-shave reminded me of the old leather suitcases. Had he taken them on *his* first trip away from home? Of course not, they weren't *that* old. Still, it made me feel good to be taking something that had been in the McGovern family for as long as I could remember.

"So long, Katydid," my dad said softly. He kissed me and his new mustache tickled my upper lip.

Before things could get any more emotional, I hopped in the back seat of the car and let Dee crawl over me so I could sit in the middle. By putting the toys and books on the floor I had just enough room. Bill started the car, we all waved until our arms got sore, and my parents looked smaller and smaller as we drove down the street. When we turned a corner and I couldn't see them anymore, I knew the trip had really begun.

The trip from Fairbanks to Long Beach Island takes about two hours. Usually, I count the minutes, but on this trip I barely noticed the time passing. That's because I was so busy taking care of Dee and Ricky. Both of them wanted my undivided attention, so I had to come up with things they both liked to do. Mostly I read picture books and went through my repertoire of children's songs.

Finally Ricky fell asleep. Dee was trying not to show how tired she was, but after we stopped at a gas station to use the bathrooms, she conked out with her head on my lap. Around that time, I noticed there was sand along the edge of the highway instead of dirt. Soon after that, we entered the New Jersey pines—miles and miles of pine tree forests—and I knew we were almost there.

Tina was driving now. Bill turned around and grinned. "Well, you finally wore them out."

"It feels like the other way around," I answered.

"We're really glad you're coming along," said Tina. "It's going to make our summer a lot more enjoyable."

"Mine too," I said, thinking about all the surfing I planned to do.

"Oh Kate," said Tina, "now that Dee's asleep, I want to tell you something." I stopped thinking about waves and surfboards and listened to Tina. She sounded worried. "We were at the YMCA pool last week," she told me, "and Dee had a real scare."

"What happened?"

"Well, I was in the adult pool and she was supposed to be in the kiddie pool, but she came over to ask me something. I guess she was walking a little too fast because she slipped and fell into the deep end. She wasn't hurt, but the lifeguard had to pull her out."

"It really frightened her," added Bill, "and now she absolutely refuses to go near the water."

I looked down at Dee, asleep with her head in my lap. She was frowning and her fists were clenched. Was she dreaming about the YMCA pool? I wondered.

"We just wanted to let you know so you'll be prepared when you take the kids to the beach," Tina explained. "We're hoping she'll get over her fears when she sees you and Ricky in the water. But if she doesn't want to swim, don't push her."

"Okay," I agreed. Just then we came to the bridge that spans the bay and connects Long Beach Island to the mainland. As we drove over the bridge, I felt as excited and impatient as a little kid. I was glad when Bill and Tina started talking to each other so I could stare out the window and think my own private thoughts.

I leaned my head out the window and breathed in the fresh ocean air. Out on the bay, sailboats and speedboats were cutting up the water. When we left the bridge we turned onto the boulevard, the main road that runs the length of Long Beach Island. All the stores were open and the sidewalks were crowded with people, most of them wearing nothing but bathing suits and sandals. I could hardly wait to put on my new suit and join them.

Then we reached Beach Haven and drove past The Curl, the surf shop where I rented my board last summer. There were boards lined up on the sidewalk and a couple of good-looking surfers were looking at them. I longed to be there with them, checking out the boards and discussing the surf conditions.

Eventually, Tina turned off the boulevard and took one of the side streets that ran down to the bay. We pulled into the driveway of a small wood-shingled house with blue shutters. Like all the other houses on the street, there was no grass in the front yard, just sand.

When Tina turned off the car, Dee and Ricky woke up. Ricky was groggy and confused, but Dee bounced up and down in her seat and shouted, "Get out, Kate! We're here! We're here!"

The rest of the afternoon was spent unpacking, playing with Dee and Ricky, and eating dinner. I barely had a chance to catch my breath until after seven o'clock. Finally, Tina started running the water for the children's baths and I told Bill I was going to walk up to the beach for a few minutes. He nodded, but didn't look up from the book he was reading. I took that as a good sign. My father would probably have asked me a million questions about where I was going, who I was going with, and exactly when I'd be home. It looked like the Bensons weren't going to be too strict.

A cool breeze was blowing as I ran up the street to the ocean side of the Island. A few people were walking on the beach and a half-dozen surfers were in the water, hoping to catch a couple more waves before sunset. I sat on the cool white sand and watched the sandpipers rushing down to the water. The air was chilly so I folded my arms around my legs and wished I had thought to change into my long pants.

Shivering there on the beach, I suddenly felt very alone. My parents and friends were miles away. I missed them, and I missed Chris too. Had I done the right thing in coming here? I wondered. Maybe I should have just stayed in Fairbanks with Chris and all our friends. Sure, it got boring sometimes, going to all the same old places with the same old gang. But at least it was familiar. In Fairbanks I was Chris's girl, but who was I in Beach Haven, New Jersey? Just a mother's helper, dragging somebody's little kids to the beach every day. How was I ever going to make any friends or have any fun?

Just then a couple of boys came out of the water, carrying their surfboards on their heads. They glanced at me as they walked past, but I was so lost in thought I barely noticed. Then I heard a voice behind me say,

"She's cute, huh?" Without thinking, I turned around. One of the boys—a tall, dark-haired guy—was looking at me, and when our eyes met, he smiled. It only lasted a second, but I managed to smile back just before he turned away.

The surfers were soon out of sight, but I was still smiling. The crashing waves had never looked more beautiful and the breeze seemed to be whispering secrets to me, secrets about the wonderful summer that lay ahead. For some reason, I wasn't worried now. I knew this was going to be a special summer. Wonderful things were going to happen, I could just feel it.

Looking up, I realized it was getting dark. The beach was almost deserted and the last surfers were paddling in. I was afraid if I didn't get back soon, the Bensons would be worried. Turning my back on the ocean, I ran up the beach and headed down the street to their house.

Chapter Three

When I woke up the next morning, it took me a few seconds to realize where I was. The tiny bedroom looked completely unfamiliar. Even my leather suitcases looked strange. But then I took a deep breath and the fresh ocean smell brought everything back. This was my first full day at the shore!

I rubbed my eyes and reached for the clock on my bedside table. Ten after six!? With a yawn, I rolled over and closed my eyes. I'd almost fallen back asleep when I realized why I was awake in the first place. Ricky was crying.

I let out a groan and dragged myself out of bed. Last night Tina had gone over my work schedule with me. I would be taking care of Dee and Ricky every day except Sunday, from the time they got up until two P.M. Unfortunately, Ricky usually woke up around six o'clock.

"This is inhuman!" I moaned as I threw on a robe and staggered down the hall.

Because I was sleeping in the room that Ricky had used last summer, his crib was set up in the playroom. The playroom is actually a little glassed-in porch that opens onto the living room. Toys covered the floor and Ricky's

18

clothes were still in an open suitcase on the floor. The morning sun shone through the windows, creating a grid of light and shadow on the rug. It was beautiful, but right then I was too tired to care.

Ricky was standing up in his crib, hugging his teddy bear and sucking his thumb. When he saw me, he smiled and said, "Katie here."

"Good morning, Ricky," I said with forced enthusiasm. I lifted him out of his crib and placed him on the floor. Now what? I wondered. Fortunately, Ricky sat down and immediately began playing with his toy trucks. Gratefully, I seized the opportunity to rest my head on his teddy bear and close my eyes.

The next thing I knew, Dee was shaking my shoulder. "You better change Ricky's diaper," she said. "He's getting the floor all wet."

I was instantly awake and expecting the worst. Had Ricky destroyed the house while I was dozing? But everything was fine. Ricky was still playing with his toys, although he *had* broken a wheel off one of his trucks. Dee had just gotten up and Bill and Tina were still asleep. It was only seven o'clock.

Ricky's pajamas were soaked and I realized I should have changed him as soon as he woke up. Despite his protests, I put a new diaper on him and forced him into some clothes. By then, Dee was dressed and demanding breakfast, so we went into the kitchen and checked out the refrigerator.

Dee wanted scrambled eggs and Ricky wanted pancakes, but I couldn't find anything except cereal and milk. They complained a lot, but finally ate it. I did too, even though I hate cold cereal.

When breakfast was over it was still only seven-thirty. There were over six hours to go until two o'clock and I realized I had never taken care of Dee and Ricky for longer than four or five hours at a time. What were we going to do all day?

"I want to go to the beach," said Dee.

"Yeah," agreed Ricky. "Beach, beach!"

I didn't have any better ideas, so I got Ricky into his bathing suit and started throwing things into a couple of knapsacks. There were so many things to take—towels, toys, books, diapers, suntan lotion, hats, juice, crackers—the list seemed endless. While I got organized, Ricky hopped around me whining, "Go now, Katie. Go, go!"

Finally, I threw one knapsack over my shoulder, hung the other on Ricky's stroller and left a note for Bill and Tina. I strapped Ricky in the stroller and called Dee.

"Where's your bathing suit?" I asked when I saw her. She was still in her shorts and shirt.

"I'm not wearing it," she said. "I'm not swimming."

"But you might want to sit by the edge of the water," I suggested. "I think you should wear it."

Dee looked like she was going to cry. She pressed her lips together and shook her head.

"Okay," I said. It was too early for a scene, and besides, I didn't want to push her. I smiled hopefully. "Everybody ready?"

It was still cool outside and the streets were mostly empty. It took a long time to get to the beach because Dee and Ricky had to pet three dogs, watch a garbage truck and pick some wildflowers. When we finally got there, I took Ricky out of his stroller and made Dee hold his hand while I carried all our junk.

It was too early for the lifeguards to be on duty, and I counted thirteen surfers in the water. If only I could have been one of them! I glanced at Dee and Ricky, making their way down the beach. They're great kids, but at that moment, babysitting was the last thing on my mind. I just wanted to grab a board and catch a couple of those perfect waves. With a sigh, I spread out our blanket and looked around.

The only other people on the beach were mothers, babysitters and children. Everyone else with any sense was undoubtedly fast asleep. I dumped all the toys out of the knapsacks and sat down. Ricky started playing with some blocks, but Dee just sat there, staring nervously at the crashing waves. Poor kid! I figured it was best not to say anything though. Instead, I took off my T-shirt and started pouring suntan oil all over me. I was wearing my new black bikini, so there was plenty of skin exposed. I got Dee to rub some lotion on my back and I put some on her too.

I was all set to lie down and watch the surfers when I noticed Ricky wasn't on the blanket. For a second I panicked, but he was only at the edge of the water, pushing his feet in the sand. Still, I figured I should stay with him.

"Come on, Dee," I said. "Let's go down with Ricky." She shook her head. "I'll give you a piggyback ride," I offered.

"I don't want to."

"Well, if you come a little closer, I'll bring you some wet sand to play with. Okay?"

That seemed to do the trick. I coaxed Dee to about ten feet away from the water and then brought her five buckets of wet sand. "Work fast," I told her. "It's already starting to dry out."

Dee began a sand castle and I returned to Ricky. He certainly wasn't afraid of the water. He was up to his waist and laughing.

Ricky's a great kid, but he's at that age known as "the terrible twos." He's so demanding and half the time, no matter what I say or do, he says no. So of course when I picked him up, he screamed, "No! No!" Then he realized I was carrying him into the deep water and he was delighted. We walked out until I was up to my chest and while Ricky splashed around in my arms, I watched the surfers and studied their moves.

After a while the lifeguards showed up and the surfers carried their boards out of the water. I looked for the dark-haired guy who had smiled at me on the beach last night, but he wasn't around. No one smiled at me today, I noticed. They probably thought Ricky was my kid and I was just a boring old mother. How depressing!

When the surfers left, I got Dee some more wet sand. She made a beautiful sand castle which Ricky eventually knocked down. That started a terrific fight but I brought out the juice and crackers and they calmed down. I even got to read my book—a fantasy called *The Snow Queen*—while Dee and Ricky played with some other kids.

At noon we gathered up our possessions and walked home. Bill and Tina were both up by then, of course, but they were working out in the former garage (now their studio). Someone had gone shopping and there was lots of food in the refrigerator so I made tuna fish sandwiches.

After lunch it was time for Ricky's nap and Dee's quiet time. It's always easy to tell when Dee and Ricky need to rest. Dee spilled her milk at lunch and Ricky fell down and bumped his head. They were irritable and contrary and by the time I put the dishes in the sink, they were both crying.

I read Ricky a story and put him in his crib with a pile of toys. He screamed bloody murder when I left, but by the time I got back to the kitchen he'd quieted down. Then I sat Dee at the table with paper and crayons while I did the dishes.

At two o'clock, Tina appeared with a big smile on her face. "How'd it go?" she asked brightly.

"Fine," I told her. It *had* gone fine, really, so I saw no point in telling her I was completely and totally exhausted. I had no idea how I could possibly live through an entire summer of babysitting Dee and Ricky. All I wanted to do was sleep!

But I had plans for this afternoon, and I wasn't going to cancel them no matter what. "Tina," I asked, "may I borrow the car?"

"Sure," she said. "What do you want it for?"

"I'm going to rent a surfboard." Tina and Bill knew I liked surfing, but I had never actually told them I planned to go surfing this summer. I didn't know if Tina had talked to my parents about it or what her feelings were on the subject. I didn't know what I'd do if she said no.

"Oh, surfing," she said. "Sure, go ahead. But bring the car back by six."

Overjoyed, I changed into my one-piece bathing suit and ran out to the car. It felt fabulous to be cruising down the boulevard with the wind in my hair and the radio turned up loud.

When I reached The Curl, I parked the car and walked over to look at the surfboards that were lined up outside. They were all shapes and colors and had one, two, or even three fins. I looked at them all, imagining which one I would buy, but when the salesman—a scruffy, middle-aged surf bum type—showed up, I had to admit I just wanted a rental board. He pulled out a plain blue twin-fin and then took me inside to pay.

Inside The Curl there were more boards, wet suits, wax, magazines and other surfing accessories. When I saw some postcards, I remembered Chris. I'd barely had a second to think of him since I'd been here, but now I felt a pang of guilt. I bought a postcard and planned to send it that night. A letter, I promised myself, would follow.

Behind the main part of The Curl there's another room where they make and repair surfboards. While I was looking at the postcards, I happened to glance back there and my heart almost stopped. A tall, terrifically good-looking guy was working on one of the surfboards. He had straight blond hair, a perfect tan and huge baby-blue eyes.

That's him! I thought. That's the guy I want to get to know this summer! But how? I couldn't very well walk up to him and say, "Looking for a girlfriend, handsome?" I tried staring at him, hoping he might at least look at me, but he just kept on working.

When the salesman finished writing up the rental agreement I paid my money and got ready to go. Then I had an idea. If I said something really brilliant, maybe the guy in the back room would hear me. Maybe he'd look up and say, "Gee, you really know a lot about surfing. What's your name?"

I looked wildly around the store and prayed for inspiration. The first thing I saw was a poster of a surfer hot-dogging across the face of a long green wave. "Is that poster of Mark Richards at the Pipeline for sale?" I asked loudly.

The salesman eyed me with a combination of amusement and disgust. "That's Matt Kechele at Sebastian Inlet," he said. "And it's not for sale."

I wanted to die! Any surfer worth his board can tell the difference between Hawaii's Banzai Pipeline and Florida's Sebastian Inlet. Flushed with embarrassment, I hurried out of the store, not even looking to see if the cute guy in the back room had heard me. Boy, I hoped not!

I put my board in the back of the station wagon and drove off to the southern end of the Island. A minute ago I'd been thinking about Chris, but now I couldn't seem to get that boy in the surf shop out of my head. He was so handsome and I was sure he was a great surfer too. If he hadn't heard my stupid question about the poster, I might still have a chance with him. Now, if I could only find a way to meet him. . . .

I stopped at the first deserted beach I came to. The waves were small and breaking from left to right. As I pulled my board from the car and walked down the beach, I could feel myself getting more and more excited. I had to force myself to stop and put on some suntan lotion. All I wanted to do was get out there! When I was completely sun-proofed, I waded into the cool water, hopped on my board and paddled out.

It was great to feel the board under me and to see the water all around. I paddled out to where the waves were breaking and sat on my board to wait for the next set. When the first wave came, I took off and as soon as I felt it rise under me, I stood up. "I'm surfing!" I cried, and immediately fell off.

That's how I spent the rest of the afternoon. I just kept catching waves, standing up, and falling off. Each time I was able to stay on a little longer though, and eventually I actually made it all the way across the face of the wave. My muscles ached and I was breathing hard, but I forced myself to surf five straight waves without wiping out. Then I dragged myself out of the water.

On the way home, I turned up the radio and thought about the guy in the surf shop. There must be hundreds of good-looking surfers on this island, I thought, and I can't even meet one. Of course, I had to admit I hadn't really tried very hard. I'd spent the morning with Dee and Ricky

and most of the afternoon by myself. The only time I'd
actually gotten within ten feet of a really handsome boy,
I'd made a fool of myself by trying to show off my nearly
non-existent knowledge of surfing.

But tomorrow, I promised myself, would be different.
There would be no more hiding out at deserted beaches. I
planned to take my board to the most crowded beach on
the whole island. That way I'd be sure to meet *someone*,
even if I had to surf right into him to do it!

Chapter Four

When Ricky woke up at 6:05 the next morning, I was able to greet him with a sincere smile. That's because I'd gone to bed at nine o'clock the night before and I was feeling pretty rested. The only problem now was my muscles. Despite three years on the high school swim team, an afternoon of surfing had left me sore. My only consolation was knowing I'd be in great shape by the end of the summer, and probably be a whiz at the 100-meter butterfly next year.

Dee and Ricky had gotten a lot of sun yesterday so today we only hit the beach for an hour or two. After that I took them to the library and we spent the rest of the morning reading and watching children's movies.

When two o'clock rolled around, I was raring to hit the beach. Bill needed the car, but he dropped me off near the popular surfing beaches at the end of the island. Even so, I had to walk about ten blocks with my surfboard under my arm. It's not all that heavy, actually, but after yesterday my shoulder muscles weren't in top condition and by the time I reached a really crowded beach, I was exhausted.

I dropped my board in the sand and plopped down on top of it. The waves were small and long today—just right for doing tricks. Everyone was out there showing off and consequently there were a lot of wipe-outs and collisions. My plan to meet someone by surfing right into him seemed frighteningly possible, and I almost wished I was back at the deserted beach I'd found yesterday.

But I'd come to meet surfers and this looked like the perfect place to do it. The beach was crawling with boys of all shapes and sizes. There were girls too, including a few knockouts in bikinis that barely covered their private parts, but I didn't see any girls surfing. Gathering up my courage, I sloshed on some suntan lotion, waxed down my board and paddled out.

When I joined the surfers that were waiting for waves, I realized I'd been right. I was the only girl in the water. Out of the corner of my eye, I could see the boys checking me out. I guess my one-piece suit proved I was there to surf, not show off my body, because no one talked to me. They just watched me and waited to see what I could do.

Naturally, I felt pretty self-conscious. Without thinking, I took off on the first wave that came along and barely had time to stand up before it broke on me and I slid off into the foam. After that, most of the guys stopped watching me and concentrated on their own surfing. It seemed I wasn't gorgeous enough to drool over and I wasn't a good enough surfer to take seriously.

I felt discouraged, but a little relieved. Now that I wasn't being stared at, I could just surf and after a while maybe I could start up a conversation with someone. If that didn't work, I'd just have to come back tomorrow wearing my skimpy black bikini. When it fell off in the water, I'd be sure to make friends.

I forced myself to slow down and wait for the good waves. Eventually, I managed to get a few long rides and I was feeling pretty good. Each time I paddled back out, I watched the other surfers and tried to learn from them. I saw when they took off and how they moved on the board to make it turn and dip. By imitating them, I managed to maneuver across the waves without wiping out or colliding into anyone. That second part was very important since every wave seemed to have at least two surfers on it vying for the best position.

I was getting pretty tired and I'd just about decided to catch one more wave and ride in when a new set of waves began. They were larger and smoother than the ones before and everyone around me started paddling like crazy to get into position. I decided to hang back though and wait for a less crowded wave. When most of the other surfers had taken off, I looked behind me and saw the wave I wanted. I flopped down on my board and started paddling, oblivious to everything except getting that wave.

"Hey you, pull back! This is my wave!"

I glanced out of the corner of my eye and saw that someone else was paddling beside me. What's he yelling about? I wondered. Every wave I'd been on that day had at least two surfers on it, sometimes more. This guy had no right to expect me to pull back. I kept on paddling and as the wave swelled under me, I stood up.

The other surfer stood up right beside me, but I noticed with satisfaction that I had the better position on the wave. It didn't seem to bother him though. He was cutting up and down the wave and showing off like crazy. I was pretty flustered—this guy was obviously a *much* better surfer than I was—but I kept looking straight ahead and concentrated on what I was doing. The last thing I wanted was to wipe-out and give this show-off an opportunity to laugh at me.

When the wave died, I started paddling in. "Not bad,"

I heard a voice say. "I never would have believed a paleface like you could be much of a surfer, but you proved me wrong."

I laughed and sat up on my board. My rival was paddling up beside me and when I took a good look at him, I almost died. It was *him*—the gorgeous guy from the surf shop! His straight blond hair glistened with water and his eyes were as blue as the sky above us. He was straddling his board with his hands resting lightly on his hips and his white swim trunks stood out against his smooth, well-tanned skin.

I felt my cheeks turning pink and I knew it wasn't from the sun. "T-thanks," I said. "But really, I'm just a beginner."

"You've got the right instincts though," he said. "You could be really good with practice and the right teacher."

He smiled warmly and I felt my pulse quicken. You! I wanted to scream. You're the right teacher! Instead, I just sat there, grinning and saying nothing at all.

"Are you going in?" he asked.

I forced myself to speak. "Yes. I'm exhausted, and if I don't put on more suntan lotion I might burst into flames."

He laughed and pushed his blond hair back from his forehead. "I'm coming in too." We waded in and dropped our boards next to my towel. "Not many girls around here surf," he said as I poured suntan lotion on my arms. "How did you get started?"

I told him about our family vacations and my two weeks of surfing last summer. I also explained about my job with the Bensons, including the fact that I was at the shore for the whole summer and planned to surf almost every day. "This is just a rental board," I added, "but I hope to buy my own surfboard soon."

"I thought I recognized that board," he said, sitting beside me on the beach towel. "I work at The Curl."

I waited miserably for him to add that he'd seen me in there yesterday, making a jerk of myself over the Matt Kechele poster, but he didn't say anything. Thank God! "How did you start surfing?" I asked.

"Oh, I live here," he told me. "My family owns a marina in Surf City and I've been surfing since I was twelve. I'm hoping to go professional next year." He took the bottle of suntan lotion out of my hands. "Turn around," he said. "I'll do your back."

The touch of his warm fingers sent shivers of pleasure down my spine. I wanted to just close my eyes and enjoy the feeling, but I was too embarrassed. "A professional surfer?" I repeated.

"It won't be easy," he said seriously. "I know that. I'll have to travel to competitions all over the world, and even if I win, the money isn't that good. But I love surfing and I've done well in the East Coast amateur contests. I want to give it a try."

Boy, was I impressed! This guy was a serious surfer, the kind you read about in surfing magazines. In a few years, I thought, they might have a poster of *him* on the wall of The Curl. And here he was beside me, rubbing suntan lotion on my back!

"All done," he said, closing the bottle and tossing it on the blanket. I turned to face him. "By the way, my name is Steve," he said. "Steve Matheson."

"Hi. I'm Kate McGovern." It seemed silly to be introducing ourselves after we'd already been talking for ten minutes. We both laughed self-consciously and Steve turned to look at the waves.

"The surf is small today," he said. "Of course, it's always small in New Jersey. You have to go to the West

Coast for the really big waves.''

"Have you been there?" I asked.

"No, maybe next year. I've been down the East Coast though. Some friends and I took a trip to Florida this past winter. There's good surf there, and some amazing surfers."

Steve and I talked for the next half-hour. He told me about his trip to Florida and about another surfing trip he took to Virginia Beach. Compared to that, I felt my end of the conversation was pretty dull, but Steve seemed interested. He asked me questions about my family and I told him about the swim team and about my adventures with Dee and Ricky.

When I finally glanced at the watch in my backpack, it was after five-thirty. "Oh no!" I cried. "I have to get home. The Bensons expect me for dinner at six."

"You still have a half-hour."

"Yeah, but I don't have a car, and it'll take more than that to walk home."

"Don't worry," Steve told me. "I'll drive you." When I tried to protest he said, "It's no problem, Kate. I was planning to leave soon anyway."

Steve's car was a beat-up white Mustang convertible. We threw the boards in the back seat and got into the front. As we took off down the boulevard, I realized my dream had come true. I was cruising down Long Beach Island with a good-looking surfer by my side. It felt terrific!

A few minutes later we were turning into the Bensons' driveway. "Thanks," I said. "This was a lot better than carrying my board down the boulevard."

"What about tomorrow?" Steve asked. "Are you going surfing?"

I felt a little breathless. "Yes," I said. "In the afternoon."

"Then let's meet at the Washington Avenue beach. It's in Beach Haven Heights. Do you know where I mean?"

I didn't know exactly, but I knew the area and I was sure I could find it. "Okay," I answered. I looked into his beautiful blue eyes and wondered what to say next.

"What time can you get there?" he asked.

"Two-thirty." I was still staring into his eyes, and he was gazing back into mine. We might have sat there all night if something hadn't broken the spell.

"Katie here!" said a little voice. Steve and I looked up to see Ricky's face pressed against the inside of the screen door.

Laughing, I got out of the car. I grabbed my board and waved as Steve backed out of the driveway. "Two-thirty at Washington Avenue," he called, and then took off in the direction of Surf City.

Ricky was on the porch now, and I leaned my board against the house and hoisted him on to my shoulders. "Horsey ride!" he cried and with a whoop of joy, we galloped off into the house.

Chapter Five

That night I decided to go to Bay Village. Bay Village is a group of stores built around a little square, and it's also a sort of teenage hangout. All the kids on the island go there to browse through the book store and craft shops, eat Belgian waffles, and meet each other.

After a morning of Dee and Ricky and an afternoon of surfing, I was exhausted, but I went anyway, mostly just to get out of the house. It wasn't that I didn't enjoy the Bensons, but for me being at the shore doesn't mean sitting around at night, reading the paper and putting the kids to bed. It means cruising the boulevard, hanging around Bay Village, seeing a movie or going to a club.

Besides, I wanted a chance to be alone with my thoughts about Steve. I wanted to replay the whole afternoon in my mind—the crazy way we met, the way his straight blond hair fell over his forehead, the sparkle in his handsome blue eyes, and the warmth in his voice when he asked, ''What about tomorrow? Are you going surfing?''

Tomorrow! That's the part I wanted to think about most of all. Should I stick with my one-piece bathing suit, I wondered, or risk wearing my bikini? Should I bring some food for us? What will we talk about? Will we be alone?

And most important of all, does he really like me?

I was thinking all these things as I walked down the boulevard toward Bay Village. It gets cool at the shore when the sun goes down, so I was wearing my jeans and a long-sleeved turquoise blouse with my fisherman's sweater tied over my shoulders. Kids were cruising their cars up and down the street with the radios blasting. I looked for Steve's white Mustang, but he didn't seem to be around.

Bay Village was really crowded that night. People were pushing into the stores and waiting in line for the restaurants. In the central square, teenagers were sitting on the benches and curbs, laughing, eating and checking each other out.

I bought a Belgian waffle with whipped cream and strawberries and looked around while I ate it. Everyone, it seemed, was with someone. There were couples walking hand in hand and lots of children with their parents. Most of the benches were filled with kids my age, but they all seemed to know each other already. They were drinking sodas and talking loudly. Every now and then someone said something that made them all laugh.

What had happened to the days when everyone came to Bay Village to make friends? I wondered. If this evening was any indication, all the teenagers on the island already knew each other. Standing there watching them all, I felt very alone.

I finished my waffle and wandered away from the square. Bay Village is right next to the bay and without really thinking about it, I found myself walking down to the beach. It was quiet there, and sitting in the sand with the dark water lapping at my feet, I let my thoughts drift back to my friends at home.

There are seven or eight of us who always hang around

together. We go to the school dances and the football and basketball games. Sometimes we spend a Saturday in New York City. In the summer, we swim at the municipal pool or drive up to the lake.

This summer, I was the only member of our gang who wasn't staying in Fairbanks, and everyone had told me how lucky I was to be getting away. I knew they were right, but right now I felt homesick. I missed hanging out at the pool with Amy and Rachel. I missed driving up to the lake with Chris. . . .

Chris. The memory of our fight after the sports banquet still lingered in my mind, stirring up a jumble of emotions that was almost impossible to untangle. Guilt, anger, longing, love—all sorts of feelings I couldn't explain. At this point, I wasn't sure if Chris was still my boyfriend, or even if I wanted him to be.

And what was Chris thinking about me? I had sent off the postcard I bought in The Curl and I knew he'd probably get it the day after tomorrow. Then what? Would he write back? Or would he rip up the card and toss it in the garbage? Actually, I wasn't sure which reaction I'd prefer. All I knew was that I was seeing Steve tomorrow, and compared to that nothing else mattered.

With a sigh, I dipped my hand in the cool water and let my thoughts turn to Steve. He seemed so self-assured and independent. Imagine driving all the way to Florida on a surfing trip! It's true I didn't know Steve very well, but he seemed so much like my idea of what a surfer should be—carefree, uninhibited, adventuresome and free. Just being around him had made me feel wonderful.

I tried to remember the way I'd felt when I first met Chris. Had it been like that? I wondered. I thought back to the night I'd first seen him play basketball. He looked so relaxed and graceful, leaping over the other players to score the winning basket. I was in seventh heaven when he asked me out for pizza after the game.

But all that seemed very long ago and far away. It was hard to imagine getting all excited over Chris now. In fact, most of the time our relationship was more like a brother and sister than a boyfriend and girlfriend. Did I still love Chris, I wondered, or was I just used to being with him? Sitting there by the water, I told myself I missed him. But did I miss him any more than I missed the rest of my friends? Probably not.

Confused and guilty, I walked back to Bay Village and wandered through the stores. When I spotted a T-shirt I thought Chris would like, I quickly bought it. It was black with silver stars sprinkled across the chest, and I knew he would look good in it.

Feeling a little better, I sat on one of the benches and listened to the music blasting from a nearby radio. Look, I told myself, you're just going surfing with Steve. It isn't even a real date, so stop feeling guilty. Besides, I reminded myself, Chris was almost two hours away, in fabulous Fairbanks. Even if I spent the whole summer with Steve, Chris would never know. And when I returned to school in September, Chris would be there waiting for me, just as if I'd never left.

Cheered by this thought, I looked through a few more stores. I bought four postcards—one for my parents, one for John, and one each for Amy and Rachel. In the bookstore, I picked up the latest copy of *Surfer* and a new fantasy novel by Anne McCaffrey. After that, I decided to head home, but on the way out of Bay Village, the bakery caught my eye. I've always loved their chocolate chip cookies, so I stopped off for one to eat on the way home.

As I walked through the door, the delicious smell of cakes and cookies filled my nose. There were about five people ahead of me, so I stood back and looked around while I waited.

I always liked the Bay Village Bakery. The dark wood walls are used to display the work of local artists and that evening they were covered with intricate macrame hangings of rope, beads and shells. Above my head, an old-fashioned fan turned just fast enough to keep the delicious smells circulating. Behind the counter, a teenage girl was . . .

Cindy Levine? I don't know why, but I couldn't believe I was really seeing someone from Fairbanks. I looked again. Yes, it was Cindy, wearing a Bruce Springsteen T-shirt and a No Nukes button pinned to her white bakery apron. Her hair was shorter than it had been at the end of school, but it was still the same Cindy Levine, straight from my hometown.

Cindy went to Fairbanks High and she was in my physics class and gym class last year. We never really knew each other though. In fact, we moved in completely different circles. My friends were mostly into school sports—swimming, basketball, football or cheerleading. We went to the pep rallies and the games and looked forward to the homecoming dance and the prom.

Cindy and her friends were completely different. They wore weird clothes and carried around records by groups like The Clash and Elvis Costello. One person in her group even had her hair dyed blue! They never went to the games or the school dances but I knew Cindy was on the student council. I'd heard her at an assembly, recruiting people for a committee on senior independent study projects.

I never knew quite what to make of Cindy and her friends. Some of the kids in my group laughed at them, but I didn't really get involved. I'd never said more than two words to any of them though, and now that I realized Cindy and I were going to be face to face in about thirty seconds, I felt completely tongue-tied.

I thought of leaving the bakery before she saw me, but something made me hesitate. I couldn't imagine spending much time with Cindy, but I was a little lonely and she was a familiar face, and . . .

"Kate McGovern!"

Cindy was grinning and looking right at me. I smiled back "Hi, Cindy. I didn't know you were coming to the shore this summer."

"Yeah. My boyfriend's brother-in-law owns this place, so he gave me a job. Pretty boring, huh? Hey, are you on vacation?"

"No," I said. "I'm babysitting for a family on West Avenue. I'm here for the whole summer."

"Far out. You know, we ought to get together. Have you been to The Club?"

"No," I answered. "What's that?"

Cindy paused to wait on another customer. "It's a dance club in Ship Bottom," she told me. "They don't serve liquor, so you don't have to be twenty-one to get in. It's a pretty cool place. My boyfriend's in the rock band that plays there every weekend. They're called The Spikes."

I pictured a bunch of lunatics with safety pins through their noses, but I didn't say anything. Then to change the subject I asked, "Can I have a chocolate chip cookie?"

"Sure," replied Cindy. "On the house." She reached down and handed me the largest cookie. "Stay and talk to me awhile, will ya? This job can be a real drag."

While I munched on the cookie, Cindy told me how she met her boyfriend, Jeep. She'd seen The Spikes perform at a rock club in New York City. She thought Jeep was

cute but she didn't know how to meet him. Finally in
desperation she threw him a Coke bottle with a message in
it. The bouncers threw her out for causing a disturbance,
but Jeep came out to find her after the show. Now she was
spending the summer with Jeep and his family in Surf
City.

There was no way I could top a story like that, but I told
Cindy about the Bensons and my summer job. I also told
her my surfing plans, but I left out any mention of Steve. I
loved thinking about him, but maybe because so little had
actually happened between us, the idea of talking about
him embarrassed me. I at least wanted to wait until tomorrow to see how things worked out.

More customers soon appeared and while Cindy waited
on them, I looked again at the macrame wall hangings. I
couldn't believe how intricate and beautiful they were. I
especially liked the ones that included shells and driftwood, and as I walked closer to look at them, I noticed a
small sign on the wall.

MACRAME WALL HANGINGS

BY

CINDY LEVINE OF FAIRBANKS, N.J.

"Cindy!" I exclaimed. "I didn't know you made
these. They're beautiful!"

Cindy grinned self-consciously. "Oh, thanks. This is
just some stuff I fool around with. I'm actually more into
sculpture. I'm doing a big piece now with plaster and car
parts. You oughta see it."

It turned out Cindy had done sculptures out of all sorts
of things—forks, guitar strings, even hair. Now she was
excited about working with car parts. One of the reasons
she formed a student council committee on senior inde-

pendent studies, she told me, was because she wanted to
do an apprenticeship with a local garage mechanic next
year.

"The student council is all for it," she explained, "but
the school board is uptight. They're supposed to vote on it
at the beginning of next year."

After all that, I hardly knew what to make of Cindy! She
was certainly different from anyone I'd ever met before
and in some ways she was even weirder than my friends or
I could have imagined. But still, I liked her. She was
friendly and funny and she seemed to like me, even
though I was obviously very different. Talking to her was
so easy, in fact, that I stayed in the bakery until closing
time.

"Gee, I better go," I said. "Do you work here every
night?"

" 'Fraid so. Two until ten every night except Monday.
How about you?"

"I work in the morning." I paused and considered.
"Maybe we can get together sometime."

"How about tomorrow morning? Would the Bensons
care if I hung out with you? I'll even bring cookies," she
added.

We arranged to meet at ten the next morning at the
beach near the Bensons' house. I knew Bill and Tina
wouldn't mind. They'd even let me have Chris over while
I was babysitting last year. As long as I took good care of
Ricky and Dee, they didn't care who I brought along.

As I left, Cindy locked the door behind me. "See you
tomorrow," she said.

I waved and started off down the boulevard. The night
had grown chilly and I was glad I'd brought my fisherman's sweater. Cars were still cruising up and down the
street, blasting their radios and whenever I heard a song I

recognized, I sang along. It felt good to be there, walking and singing and breathing in the cool ocean air. And tomorrow I would be seeing Cindy and surfing with Steve. I smiled and walked a little faster. The summer, I decided, was shaping up just fine.

Chapter Six

The next morning I was at the beach with Ricky and Dee by nine o'clock. I told them Cindy was coming and as usual when one of my friends came to visit, they were all excited. I think they like the idea of having someone new to show off for.

Cindy showed up at ten, wearing a one-piece fake leopard-skin bathing suit. It was purple and black with only one strap, making her look like a refugee from a Tarzan movie. Cindy is short and cute and with all her clothes on, she borders on plump. In that bathing suit, though, she looked great—almost voluptuous—and I felt a little jealous. I have a swimmer's body—a flat chest and muscular shoulders—and I've often wished I had more of Cindy's soft curviness.

"One more month at that bakery and I'll be the size of a whale," said Cindy, flopping down next to me on the blanket. "I can't resist the doughnuts." She poked herself in the stomach. "My bathing suit barely fits."

"Are you kidding? You look great," I said. She frowned and I added, "At least you don't look like Arnold Schwarzenegger!" I flexed my biceps and Cindy laughed.

Dee and Ricky had been chasing each other around the

beach, but when they saw Cindy they came back. Dee is always shy with strangers, but Ricky knows no fear. When I introduced Cindy, he grabbed her hand and said, "Come swim!"

Cindy jumped up before I could say anything. "Lead the way, young Richard." She looked at me and added, "Don't worry. I have two little sisters and a little brother. I'm used to this."

I was glad to see Cindy and Ricky splashing around in the water together. For one thing, it gave me a few minutes alone with Dee for the first time since we arrived at the shore. For another, it kept Cindy occupied. Despite our good conversation last night, I still felt a little uncomfortable at the thought of spending time with her. I liked her, and yet her stories about her boyfriend and the car parts sculpture made me nervous. For one thing, I wasn't completely sure she wasn't just putting me on. And if she wasn't, then I didn't know what to think. Was she just trying to shock people or did she really take herself seriously?

While Cindy played tag with Ricky, I told Dee about surfing. I figured if she heard about all the fun I had in the water, she might loosen up. She listened intently, but when I asked her if she wanted to go swimming with me, she pursed her lips and shook her head. She did agree to walk along the water's edge though, and that was the closest she'd been so far. We held hands and collected shells until Ricky ran up and tagged me. "You're it!" he cried, urging Dee and me to join the game.

After fifteen minutes of that, we all collapsed exhausted onto our towels. Cindy produced cookies from a bag and while Dee and Ricky munched I said, "Is this your first summer at the shore?"

"Around here it is. My family used to go to Ocean City,

but Jeep's family always comes here. They have a house in Surf City.''

''Is Jeep his real name?''

Cindy giggled. ''Naw, it's Howard, but don't call him that. He hates it. People call him Jeep because he drives one. It's an old Army surplus jeep, painted pink.''

''Oh.'' I hardly knew what to say. I felt so ridiculously normal compared to Cindy and her friends, and for the first time in my life, normal seemed synonymous with dull. I wanted to be able to tell Cindy something exciting, something special about me. Without thinking, I said the first thing that came to my mind. ''I have a date with a surfer today. His name is Steve and he's really good.''

Cindy looked up. ''Not Steve *Matheson*,'' she said.

''Yes. Why?''

Cindy looked awed. ''He's the best surfer on the Island,'' she said. ''Maybe in all of New Jersey.''

''How do you know that?'' I asked, feeling a little lightheaded. ''I didn't know you were into surfing.''

''I'm not, but Jeep surfs a little. We saw Steve on the beach one day and Jeep pointed him out. Wow, Kate, how did you meet him?''

I felt I must be glowing with happiness. Not only was I going to spend the afternoon with the best surfer in all of New Jersey, but he had told me that *I* had the potential to be an excellent surfer too. No longer hesitant to talk about him, I told Cindy the whole story of how Steve and I met. If I was afraid Cindy would be uninterested, I soon realized I had nothing to worry about.

''That's great!'' she exclaimed. ''What a cool way to meet someone. You really have self-confidence, Kate. I would have just jumped off my surfboard and let him have the wave.''

''I don't know, Cindy. It seems to me you're the one

with self-confidence. I would never have the nerve to throw a message in a bottle to someone I liked.''

Cindy laughed. ''I was scared to death. I usually am, but if something really matters to me, I just force myself to do it.'' Cindy spoke more softly now, and she was looking down at her hands. ''I'd give anything to be as together and normal as the kids you hang around with, but I can't help it. My sculpture is important to me, even if the rest of the world thinks I'm crazy.''

''*I* don't,'' I said firmly. I meant it too. I knew now that Cindy wasn't putting me on, and she wasn't trying to shock me either. She was just being herself. Sure, she was a little kooky around the edges, but deep down inside, I had the feeling we were a lot alike. ''Maybe you envy the kids I hang out with,'' I said, ''but the only reason they tease you is because they wish they could be creative too. At least I do.''

Cindy looked up and for a second we both smiled. ''Time for a game,'' she announced suddenly. She turned to face Dee and Ricky. ''Kate and I are bucking broncos and you have to try and ride us.''

Cindy and I leapt to our hands and knees and bucked furiously while Dee and Ricky tried to throw themselves on our backs. We laughed and played until lunchtime, and then Cindy had to go home.

At two o'clock that afternoon, I went to my room and got ready to meet Steve at the Washington Avenue beach. I was tempted to wear my bikini, but reason prevailed and I finally slipped into my one-piece with the turquoise and black stripes. After all, I reminded myself, I was going surfing, not trying out to be Miss New Jersey.

I started to pull on a T-shirt but stopped as I lifted my arms above my head. The skin on my shoulders felt tight and uncomfortable, and when I looked in the mirror, my worst fears were confirmed. I was getting a terrible sunburn.

Cursing silently, I lifted my hair off my shoulders and took a good look. My back was okay, but my shoulders were definitely pink and my nose was already a bright cherry red. I couldn't believe I'd been at the shore less than a week so far. At this rate, I thought miserably, I'll be charbroiled in a month!

There was only one solution, and it was extremely depressing. First of all, I covered my shoulders with first aid cream. Then I carefully put on my T-shirt and a pair of white jeans. The T-shirt would have to stay on all day, even in the water. Finally—and this was the worst of all—I coated my nose with a heavy layer of Noxzema. It looked ridiculous, of course, but my nose was especially susceptible to sunburn and without the Noxzema I knew I'd have blisters by the end of the day.

When I got to the Washington Avenue beach, I saw Steve's car in the parking lot. Miserably, I lugged my board down the beach, dreading the moment when he would see my gloppy white nose and laugh hysterically.

Steve was lying facedown on the sand with his eyes closed, and when I dropped my board next to him, he looked up. He didn't laugh though. He just smiled and said, "Poor Kate. Sunburned already."

I sat down and sighed sadly. "The curse of the McGoverns," I said. "Only my father is exempt." I pulled my T-shirt off my shoulder and added, "Here too."

"Well, you better keep the T-shirt on. I tan easily, but I've had my share of sunburn. By August, I'll have my nose covered too."

I was so thankful to Steve for not teasing me that I could

have kissed him. Instead I looked out at the water and asked, "Have you been out today?"

"Yeah, it's not much. Small and choppy. But let's go out anyway. I want to show you how to make your turns better."

We stood up and carried our boards into the water. There were only a few people on the beach, but I hoped they were all staring at us. I was so proud to be with Steve. He looked terrific with his silky blond hair flopping down the back of his neck and the muscles on his tanned shoulders tensing under the weight of his surfboard.

We paddled out and took off together on the first decent wave. Steve called out instructions while we surfed. "Move up to the nose," he'd say and I'd struggle to stay on as the front of my board dipped forward. "Now bend your knees and lean right!" More often than not, I would be left treading water while Steve surfed on, tearing up the wave with his incredible hot dog maneuvers.

I was getting tired, but I didn't want to admit it. Luckily though, Steve suggested we paddle in. "You learn fast," he said when we were back on the beach. He sat in the sand and let the sun dry him off, but I used a towel and then applied a new layer of suntan oil.

"Thanks. I was always pretty good at water sports, things like swimming, sailing or waterskiing. I think I get that from my father."

"And what do you get from your mother?" he asked.

"This," I replied, holding up a lock of my damp red hair. "And the white skin and freckles."

"I like it," said Steve. "I like your eyes too." He leaned forward and gazed intently at my eyes. "Gray, green, and a hint of yellow. Like a cat."

Steve was only inches away and I could almost feel the

heat radiating between us. "Meow," I said, and then felt ridiculous. I sounded like Ricky making silly animal noises.

Steve laughed softly and turned away from me. He produced two cans of soda from a cooler and handed me one. "Here, little kitten," he said. "Have a drink."

While we gulped down the bubbly soda, I asked Steve to tell me more about his surfing trips down the coast.

"The best trips are yet to come," he said. "What I really want to do is go to California. If I got a part-time job there, I could spend the rest of my time surfing. I could turn professional out there and then surf my way around the world on the pro circuit." Steve was staring out at the water with a faraway look in his eyes. Obviously, this was something he took very seriously.

"What kind of job would you get?" I asked.

"I don't know. Maybe in a surf shop. I'm good at repairing boards and I'm interested in building them too."

"And what about school?" I asked.

Steve turned to look at me. "That's what my parents want to know," he said. "I just graduated from high school, and now they want me to go to Ocean County College."

"You could go to school in California," I suggested.

"That's what I told them. I could go out and get a job, and then go to school part-time. Or if I did well as a pro, I could wait and go to school later. I think I want to go to college eventually, but surfing is more important right now. Surfing comes first."

"I know," I said, and I meant it. Even though I was just a beginner, I could understand the lure of surfing. It wasn't just a sport; it was a way of life. For someone like Steve, it was everything.

Steve reached out and laid a warm hand on my arm. "I had a feeling you'd understand. From the first minute I saw you in The Curl, I . . ."

"You saw me that day?" I asked incredulously. I could feel myself blushing and I wanted to sink into the sand. "I made such a fool of myself over that Matt Kechele poster."

"Don't be so hard on yourself," he said. "The point is, you were interested. Do you know how many girls around here surf?" I shook my head. "Almost none," he said. "You're different. You're special."

You're special too, I wanted to say. You're so handsome, so kind, so different from anyone I've ever met. But all I managed was, "Thanks, Steve."

"Kate," he asked, "what are you doing this Sunday?"

"Nothing as far as I know."

"Great. Let's drive up to Barnegat Light. We can surf and have a picnic. What do you think?"

Suddenly, unbidden, Chris's face appeared in my mind and I remembered our first real date. It was on a Sunday, a week after the first time I saw him play basketball. We had a picnic in the park outside of Fairbanks. It had been a wonderful day, and the real beginning of our relationship.

That was almost two years ago, and now I was being asked out by someone new. Should I go? I wondered. As far as I knew, Chris and I were still going steady. And that meant I was cheating on him, going out with Steve behind his back.

"Well," I began, "I-I don't know . . ."

Suddenly, Steve was on his knees, lunging at my waist. With a shout, he jumped up and threw me over his shoulder. "Forget it, Kate, you don't have any choice," he cried. "If you say no, I'll just come over Sunday and carry you away!"

I laughed and tried to struggle free, but Steve held me tight. "Ste-eve!" I threatened, trying to sound angry. Secretly though, I was charmed. Steve really liked me and he wasn't afraid to show it. He was so different from Chris, who saw me only as his girl, sure and steady. I certainly couldn't imagine *him* picking me up and carrying me away.

"Okay, okay, you win!" I cried. "We'll go on a picnic on Sunday."

Gently, Steve lifted me off his shoulder and lowered me to the sand. He smiled and lightly kissed the tip of my Noxzema-covered nose. "I knew you'd see it my way," he said.

Chapter Seven

That Saturday, Tina came into the kitchen while I was feeding the kids lunch. "Two letters for Kate," she said, "and one for Dee and Ricky from Grandma." While Tina read the kids their letter, I looked at mine. One from my mother and one from Chris. I put the letter from Chris in my pocket and opened the one from my mom.

My mother's letter said that John was coming home to visit at the end of the month and bringing along his new girlfriend. Mom and Dad were going into the city to see a Broadway musical next weekend and planning a trip to the Poconos the weekend after that. The end of the letter was typically Mom. "We miss you," she wrote. "Are you getting enough sleep? Be sure to take a sweater when you go out at night. And remember, Katydid, there's other food in the world besides hamburgers and pizza. Think vegetables!" Good old Mom.

I waited until I was alone in my room to read the letter from Chris. It was printed in pen on a piece of notebook paper. He thanked me for the postcard and told me about his job, painting houses with his dad. He mostly worked with another guy named Ted, a college student whom he liked. They were painting a huge apartment building on

Beetle Street and getting a kick out of waving to all the tenants through the windows.

"Kate," he wrote at the end of the letter, "I hope you aren't still mad at me. I'm not mad at you and I want you to have a great summer. I'll come visit as soon as I can. I want to walk along the beach with you, kiss you underwater, and see you in your new black bikini (Amy told me you bought one!). I'll bet you're a knockout!"

I folded up the letter and put it in the bottom drawer of my bureau. I thought of Chris, balancing on a wobbly ladder in the boiling hot sun while I sprawled on the beach with a handsome blond surfer. Boy, did I feel guilty!

Still, the thought of not seeing Steve again barely crossed my mind. I felt drawn to him, excited by him, maybe even in love with him. On the other hand, I reminded myself, maybe it was just a summer crush. Maybe by the end of August I'd be sick to death of Steve and eager to run home to Chris. Maybe. But how would I know, unless I kept on seeing Steve? Obviously, I wouldn't. Encouraged by that brilliant bit of logic, I temporarily forgot about Chris.

I had already told Bill and Tina that I was going out with Steve on Sunday. They were very relaxed about the whole thing, but they wanted to meet Steve before we left. When he called Saturday to finalize the plans, I took Tina's suggestion and invited him over for breakfast on Sunday. Bill would make pancakes and everyone could get acquainted.

When I opened my eyes on Sunday morning, I realized I'd been dreaming about Steve. In the dream, Steve and I were surfing together on the same surfboard. We were doing all kinds of amazing tricks, moving together in perfect synchronization across a gleaming green wave. It felt terrific until I looked down at the water and realized there was someone there. It was Chris, thrashing around and calling for help. That's when I woke up.

The dream gave me an uneasy feeling, but I was determined to put it aside. This was my day with Steve, I told myself, and nothing was going to spoil it. First I took a shower and washed my hair. I brushed it out in front of the mirror and then put some first aid cream on my shoulders and face. My sunburn looked a lot better and I optimistically decided I could dispense with the Noxzema for today.

Throwing caution to the wind, I put on my black bikini. I knew it was dangerous, considering Steve and I planned to go surfing, but I hadn't gotten to wear it yet and I wanted to look my best. Over my suit I wore a green and white striped T-shirt and short cut-off jeans. When I was dressed, I walked to the nearest open store and bought some grapes, apples and bananas. Steve had told me he would bring drinks and sandwiches and I had offered to bring some fruit and the dessert—chocolate brownies I'd baked last night.

By the time Steve was supposed to show up, Dee and Ricky were running through the house in a state of wild excitement. I just hoped Steve liked kids. I also hoped Dee and Ricky didn't blurt out anything about Chris. I thought of warning them, but then I decided against it. Mentioning Chris's name would probably just put the thought in their heads, and then they would be sure to say something embarrassing.

When the doorbell rang, everyone except Bill ran to the door. He was in the kitchen, mixing the pancake batter. Steve walked through the door grinning. He looked terrific in his blue polo shirt and cut-off jeans and his blond hair was combed neatly off his forehead. He was intro-

duced to everyone and led into the kitchen where we all sat
at the table and started on coffee and orange juice.

If I'd wondered what we would all talk about, I needn't
have worried. Dee and Ricky kept up a steady stream of
chatter about their toys, their activities, and the food we
were eating. Fortunately, Steve seemed to like kids. He
listened patiently to everything Dee and Ricky said, and
even asked questions. And luckily for me, the kids
seemed too thrilled with Steve to even remember Chris.

When they finally could get a word in, Bill and Tina
talked too. Steve told them his parents owned the Matheson Marina in Surf City and that he had two married
sisters. Tina asked where we were going and when we
planned to be back. Then they talked about the cheapest
place to buy a sailboat and the best areas of the bay to sail
it.

I barely said a word during breakfast, but I didn't mind.
I just wanted to watch Steve and listen to him talk. He had
a cute way of shrugging his shoulders when he was uncer-
tain of something, and when he was thinking he rested his
chin in the palm of his left hand. Every now and then he
glanced over at me and smiled by lifting just one corner of
his mouth.

After breakfast, we put the food and my surfboard into
Steve's car and drove off down the boulevard toward the
other end of the Island. "I'm stuffed!" exclaimed Steve.
"How are we ever going to eat lunch?"

"I don't know. We may have to call it dinner instead."

We soon left Beach Haven and drove through Brant
Beach and Ship Bottom. When we hit Surf City, Steve
turned off the boulevard and drove along the bay. We
passed a large marina and Steve said, "There it is. Matheson's Folly."

"Do you live there too?" I asked.

"Yeah, upstairs above the tackle shop."

"What's it like in the winter?"

"Cold, windy and beautiful. Sometimes it's lonely too, but the winter kids all know each other. We hang out together, and there's always something going on at the high school."

We soon arrived at Barnegat Light and pulled into the parking lot. The lighthouse, a typically scenic red and white structure, is at the northern tip of the island overlooking Barnegat Inlet. Steve grabbed our surfboards, I took the food and towels, and we staggered down to the beach.

After spreading out the towels and breaking out the suntan lotion, we stripped down to our bathing suits. "Wow!" said Steve softly. "You look terrific!" He chuckled and added, "But there's a lot more of you to get sunburned now. You better let me take care of that."

This time I closed my eyes and sat quietly as Steve spread the suntan oil over my back. It felt wonderful and now I was sure that wearing my bikini had been the right thing. When he was finished, Steve flopped on his stomach and said, "Go ahead." Hesitantly, I squeezed some lotion on his back and began rubbing it in. His warm skin and strong muscles felt good beneath my hands.

When I was finished, I lay down beside him. "Tell me more about what you do around here in the winter," I said.

"Sometimes my dad and I go fishing," he replied. "Or I go with some friends to a movie on the mainland. There're dances and games at the high school, of course. And last year I spent a lot of time at Lisa's house."

"Lisa?"

Steve rolled over to look at me. "I'm sorry. I didn't

mean to mention her. She was my girlfriend, but we broke up.''

''Oh, I'm sorry.''

''Thanks, but I think it was for the best. Lisa really didn't understand me. She wanted me to marry her and work at the marina with my dad. She didn't understand about surfing. She thought it was just something for kids, something I would outgrow.''

I wasn't sure what to say, but before I could think of anything, Steve asked, ''How about you? Do you have a boyfriend back home?''

What was I going to say? My mind was racing. Should I tell him about Chris? And if I did, would Steve feel differently about me? I gazed into Steve's sky blue eyes and said evenly, ''I had one, but we broke up too.''

''What happened?''

I told Steve about the fight Chris and I had had after the sports banquet. The only difference was I made it sound even worse than it had really been, and I told him Chris had yelled, ''That's it! We're through!'' before he got into his car.

''What a creep,'' said Steve sympathetically.

''Oh well, it was probably for the best,'' I replied, caught up in my own story.

After that we carried our boards down the beach until we found a good spot for surfing. We spent the next two hours surfing, swimming and body surfing. And miracle of miracles, my bikini didn't fall off! When we finally returned to the beach, we were starving. We dug into the deli sandwiches and sodas Steve had brought, and then finished up with the brownies and the fruit.

''That was great,'' said Steve, stretching out on his towel. ''I loved those brownies. Now if only we were in Hawaii, everything would be perfect.''

"Hawaii?"

"Yeah. We could camp out on the beach and eat pine-apples for breakfast. We'd surf all day and then fall asleep under the stars."

"Sounds great!" I said, getting into the fantasy.

Steve had that faraway look in his eyes. "That's only the beginning," he said. "Then we'd head for Australia. There's great surf there. After that, South Africa and maybe France. We'd surf our way around the world!"

I laughed, but secretly, I was thrilled. Steve's fantasy was so wild, so romantic, so exotic! And he wasn't talking about doing it alone. He was talking about us. Steve and me, surfing around the world! But it was just a joke, wasn't it? "Okay," I said, waiting to see if he'd laugh. "When do we start?"

Steve smiled, but he didn't laugh. "First things first. I'll enter the Long Beach Island Championships in August and see how I do. I took a third last year, but a first would really give me some power on the East Coast. Then on to California and the big time."

I sat up. "I didn't know there was a surf contest held here."

"You bet. I took a first place in the junior division three years ago. You know, Kate, you ought to enter."

I laughed. "Me? You must be kidding!"

Steve sat up and took my hands. "Well, I'm not," he said firmly. "With your talent and my coaching, you'd do fine. You've been on a swim team so you know how to compete. You just—Kate, stop laughing. I'm serious!"

But I couldn't help it. Partly, I was laughing at the idea of my entering the Long Beach Island Championships. I mean, I was just a beginner. There was no doubt in my mind I'd make a fool of myself. Also, I guess I was laughing because I was so happy. I was sitting there next to Steve and he was actually holding my hand. It felt so wonderful. I just had to laugh.

"All right," said Steve menacingly. "You asked for it." He jumped on me and pinned my shoulders against the sand.

"You forget I have a big brother," I said, struggling against him. "I'm used to this." I grabbed his elbows and pushed until his arms bent. Then I rolled out from under him and jumped up. "You can't catch me!" I shouted, running down the beach. A minute later we were both in the water, laughing and splashing in the waves.

After more swimming and surfing, Steve and I gathered up our things and headed for home. As we pulled into the Bensons' driveway Steve said, "I'm going to be away for a few days. I'm driving down to Virginia Beach with a couple of guys from The Curl. We have to pick up some custom boards from a designer down there, but we should be back by the weekend. Do you want to do this again next Sunday?"

"Sure," I said, trying not to jump up and down with joy. "That would be great."

I started to get out of the car, but Steve held my arm and pulled me closer. "I had a terrific time today," he said softly. He kissed me lightly on the lips and I felt his warm breath against my cheek. Then he drew back and smiled.

"Me too," I almost gasped. Joyfully, I got out of the car and grabbed my board. "Next Sunday!" I called, as Steve backed out of the driveway. I waved until his white Mustang turned the corner and disappeared from sight.

Chapter Eight

Bill and Tina and I were sitting around the living room one night, reading and talking. Dee and Ricky had just gone to bed and the house was refreshingly quiet.

"Let me show you the new idea I'm working on," said Tina. "It's a calendar." She pulled out some pen and ink sketches and handed them to me. "Here's January." The drawing showed a frozen pond with children skating on it. It was nighttime with a full moon in the sky. "What do you think?" she asked.

"It's beautiful! How far have you gotten?"

"Through May. I thought for the summer months I'd draw some shore scenes. Maybe a sketch of you and the kids at the beach."

I was about to answer when the phone rang. Tina put down her sketches and went into the kitchen. A moment later she called, "Kate, it's for you."

I ran into the kitchen, expecting to hear Steve's voice, telling me he was back from Virginia Beach. Or maybe Cindy. A couple of people were sick at the bakery and she was afraid she'd have to work tomorrow instead of spending the morning with me.

I picked up the receiver. "Hello?"

"Hi, Kate! It's me!"

I knew instantly who it was. You can't talk to someone almost every day for two years without recognizing his voice. "Hi, Chris," I answered. "How are you?"

"Okay, but Kate, I miss you. And listen, I've got good news. I'm driving down to see you this Sunday!"

"Oh." I knew I was supposed to sound excited, but how could I? Sunday was already promised to Steve. We were going to spend the day together, surfing, swimming and eating a picnic lunch. How could I tell Steve I had to cancel our picnic to spend the day with Chris?

"I can't wait to see you," Chris was saying. "After you left, I started thinking about our fight, and I realized I was wrong. You had a chance to go to the shore this summer, and it was only natural you'd want to take it. I was just being pigheaded."

"T-that's okay," I managed.

"No, it isn't. I've been too possessive, and I'm going to stop. At least I'm going to try. We can talk about it on Sunday, okay?"

What could I say? Chris was being so nice, so understanding. He was trying so hard to see my point of view. How could I tell him I was seeing another boy—a handsome surfer, just as he had predicted. "Could you come on Saturday?" I asked.

"No way. We're painting the firehouse. Besides, I thought you had to work on Saturdays."

"Oh yeah, I forgot."

"Kate, are you okay?" Chris asked. "How's your job working out?"

"Fine," I said. "Just fine. Look, I'll see you on Sunday, okay?"

I could practically hear Chris grinning. "Great. You can expect me around ten. And Kate, I miss you."

''Me too,'' I muttered, and hung up.

Well, I thought miserably, so much for my picnic with Steve. With only a brief goodnight to Bill and Tina, I wandered into my room and flopped down on my bed. I had some serious thinking to do.

First of all, I had to figure out what to tell Steve when he got back from Virginia Beach. The truth, I quickly decided, was out of the question. ''Sorry I can't see you on Sunday, Steve, but my steady boyfriend from home is showing up. Yes, I know I told you we broke up, but, well, uh . . .'' Forget it!

No, the only thing to do was to lie to Steve, just this once. Then when I saw Chris on Sunday I'd bring everything out in the open. I'd tell him I was seeing someone else and that we had to break up. I knew it wouldn't be easy breaking up with Chris, but it had to be done, and telling him in person would at least be more honest than writing him a letter or telling him over the phone.

But did I really want to break up? I honestly didn't know. I still liked Chris, I knew that, but as far as I could tell in the short time we'd known each other, I liked Steve even better. Chris was steady, reliable, dependable. In a word, boring. Steve, on the other hand, was exciting, adventuresome, wild and free.

Of course, it did occur to me that ''wild and free'' might not be the best qualities to look for in a boyfriend. Maybe Steve only saw me as a brief fling, one of many girls he would date this summer. If I broke up with Chris now, I might be left high and dry when I returned to Fairbanks in September.

Still, I decided, I was willing to take that chance. Just to be with Steve—to surf beside him, to rub suntan lotion over his broad back, to feel his lips against mine—was worth the risk. Dreaming of Steve, I got undressed and slipped into bed. The night was cool and I pulled the covers up to my chin. A few minutes later I was asleep.

Steve didn't call until Saturday. "We hung around to do some surfing," he said. "Then when I got back, I had to put in overtime to catch up on all my work at The Curl."

I took a deep breath. "Steve," I said, "there's a problem about Sunday. Bill and Tina have to drive back to Fairbanks for the day and they need me to babysit."

"Darn! Well, maybe I can come over and see you."

I hadn't expected Steve to say that. "No," I answered quickly. "A whole day of Dee and Ricky would drive you nuts. Besides, I want to see you alone."

Steve laughed softly. "Okay. How about tonight? We could go to The Club."

That was exactly what I was hoping to hear. I knew Cindy would be there, and I was dying for her to meet Steve. Also, The Spikes would be playing and Cindy could introduce us to Jeep. "Great!" I told Steve. "I'd love to go. And I'm really sorry about Sunday."

"That's okay. I'll be over at eight. So long, little kitten."

Little kitten! Well, it was true that when Steve was near I wanted to purr with delight. I hung up the phone and hurried to my room to pick out something to wear. I had just about decided on white jeans and a white halter top, when Tina stuck her head around the door and asked, "No surfing today?"

"Oh, Tina, I was just going to come find you. I'm going out to The Club tonight with Steve. Is that okay?"

"Sure," said Tina, and then almost to herself she added, "and I guess it's up to me to decide when you should come home, isn't it?"

"Well, I—"

Tina laughed. ''I'm just not used to this. I spend all day telling Ricky not to put sand in his mouth and reminding Dee to share her toys. It's a whole different world.''

''I guess Dee and Ricky don't go on many dates yet,'' I teased.

''No.'' Tina laughed. ''Hardly any. I consider having you here a sort of practice run. It's good experience for when I have my own teenagers.'' Then she added, ''How about one o'clock? Does that sound like a reasonable curfew?''

''Sure,'' I replied as casually as I could. My mother, I knew, would have said midnight.

''Okay. Well, I'm off to the beach to meet Bill and the kids. See you for dinner.''

Tina left and I hurried off to wash my hair.

Steve arrived at eight, looking slender and handsome in jeans, a black shirt and a white vest. I was wearing a little makeup—mostly to highlight my eyes—and my white jeans and halter top with my favorite jacket. It's brown suede with fringe and probably the wildest piece of clothing I own. I figured it would be perfect for The Club.

When we got in the car, Steve turned on the radio and we cruised slowly down the boulevard toward Ship Bottom.

''How was your trip?'' I asked.

''Great. This guy we went to see is making some amazing boards. He's got one model that's custom designed for radical maneuvers in small surf. If I can convince The Curl to sponsor me in the Long Beach Island Championships, I'm going to use that board.''

''Speaking of boards,'' I said, ''I'm saving up my money so I can buy one. Will you help me pick it out?''

''Sure, and I can get you a discount at The Curl. We can look next week, okay?''

Steve turned off the boulevard and drove into the parking lot of a nondescript cinder block building. I wouldn't have known it was The Club except for two things: a small neon sign above the door and the loud rock music that blasted into the parking lot and practically shook the cars.

We got out of the car and Steve put his arm around me. There were a few other kids walking through the parking lot and I hoped they all saw us. This was my first real date with Steve and I wanted the whole world to know we were together.

"I hope you like to dance," said Steve, leading me into The Club.

"Absolutely," I answered happily. Chris had always been a reluctant dancer. He liked the slow numbers, but I could never convince him to let loose on the fast songs.

Steve, I soon learned, was completely different. As soon as we got in the door, he checked my jacket and led me on to the crowded dance floor. We were dancing to the pulsating music before I even had a chance to look around.

Steve was a great dancer. He didn't do anything flashy or unusual but he had a relaxed, graceful way of moving that reminded me of his surfing. I tried to match my movements to his, just like in the dream I'd had where we were surfing together on the same board.

While we danced, I looked around. The room was large and open, with chairs in the corners and a bar against one wall. The rest of the space was used as a dance floor and most of it was filled with teenagers, jumping and twisting to the steady beat. There must have been a hundred kids in there, dancing, talking or just sitting around drinking Cokes. The walls were painted black and hung with strings of Christmas lights and the ceiling was covered with flashing multicolored neon.

The music all seemed to be prerecorded and I wondered if the Spikes would really be performing tonight. I also wondered how I was going to find Cindy in such a huge crowd. Fortunately, I didn't have to worry. Steve and I were heading toward the bar for a Coke when someone tapped my shoulder.

"Hey, you made it!" It was Cindy, wearing black leather pants and a faded black T-shirt. She was holding hands with a tall, skinny boy dressed in the same outfit. "This is Jeep," she said proudly, throwing her arm around his waist.

I introduced Steve and we all exchanged greetings. Jeep had short black hair and a cute face and when he smiled I noticed he wore braces. He seemed shy and a little nervous, not at all the way I imagined a member of a rock band would be.

"Are you playing tonight?" I asked him.

"Yes," he said so softly that I had to lean forward to hear him. "In a few minutes." He pointed to a small stage I hadn't noticed before, crowded with amplifiers and instruments.

Steve left to get Cokes and I noticed he stopped every few feet to talk to someone. He seemed to know everyone, and I wished I was with him, so all his friends would be sure to see us together. I wondered how he would introduce me, and I imagined him putting his arm around me and saying, "This is my girlfriend, Kate." At least that's what I hoped he'd say.

When Steve came back he and Jeep launched into a discussion about surfing. Cindy pulled me aside and asked, "Do you like Jeep?"

"Yes," I told her. "He's cute too. What instrument did you say he plays?"

"The drums." She grinned. "He sits at the very back of the stage, you know. I really had to throw that bottle hard."

I laughed. "And do you like Steve?"

"Oh, yeah. He's a real hunk. I could definitely see you two surfing off into the sunset together."

"I wish!" I lowered my voice. "But first I have to do something about Chris. He's coming to visit tomorrow and I'm going to tell him I want to break up."

Cindy knew all about Chris. Around Fairbanks High we were a hot item, probably the longest-running steady couple in the school. Cindy patted my shoulder. "Good luck," she said sympathetically. "And call me tomorrow night to tell me how it went."

Jeep soon left to join the other Spikes and Cindy went with him. As a girlfriend of one of the band members, she was allowed backstage. Steve and I finished our Cokes and returned to the dance floor. We danced to two or three fast songs and then a slow number began.

Steve smiled and reached out to take my hands. Slowly, he pulled me toward him and took me in his arms. My cheek rested against his shoulder and my arms were around his waist. As we swayed to the romantic music, I could feel the strong muscles of his back moving beneath my hands.

Steve turned his head so his cheek was against mine. I could smell his cologne and feel his soft hair brushing against my forehead. I was glad we weren't holding hands because I was sure mine were sweating like crazy. In fact, I was so excited that my heart seemed to be beating right out of my chest. I wondered if Steve could feel it.

"This is nice," he whispered in my ear.

"Yes," I whispered back, boldly giving his earlobe a quick kiss.

He squeezed me gently and we continued dancing. When the song ended, I reluctantly moved out of Steve's arms, but before we could even look at each other, a voice cried, ''Hey everybody, we're The Spikes!''

I turned to face the stage as the band launched into its first song. It was fast and loud with a chorus that sounded like, ''We're in rock and roll reform school tonight!'' At the back of the stage sat Jeep, pounding away on his drums. He was grinning happily and looked much more at ease than he had when we talked to him. The rest of the band consisted of a bored-looking bass player and two enthusiastic guitarists who stood behind the microphones to sing, but ran to the edge of the stage to play their guitar solos. All of them wore black leather pants and black T-shirts.

Some people were dancing and some were pressed up against the stage, watching the band. Steve and I listened for a while and then rejoined the dancers. The Spikes' music wasn't big on variety, but it was perfect for dancing. The more we danced though, the hotter, sweatier and more exhausted we felt. Finally, Steve leaned forward and said, ''I need a rest. What do you say we get out of here?''

''Sure, but let me say good-bye to Cindy first.''

While Steve went to retrieve my jacket, I made my way through the crowd, looking for Cindy. I finally found her sitting on the edge of the stage, clapping her hands and singing along. ''Hey, Kate!'' she called when she saw me. ''Can you dig it?''

''Yeah!'' I yelled back. ''I like it a lot!'' It was too noisy to say much more, so I just shouted, ''If I don't see you later tonight, I'll call you tomorrow.''

''Okay!'' Cindy waved and went back to singing and I left to meet Steve. I found him by the door, talking and laughing with three other boys.

''Kate,'' Steve said when he saw me, ''I want you to meet my surfing buddies, Mark, Chuck and T.J. We went to Florida together last year.''

The boys smiled and I said hi. "Kate is a good surfer,"
Steve told them. "I'm trying to convince her to enter the
Championships."

"Go for it," said Mark. "We need some female surfers
around here."

"Debbie Beacham, watch out!" said T.J.

Debbie Beachman is probably the best woman surfer in
the world. "Believe me," I said self-consciously, "I'm
not in her league."

"Soon, " said Steve, putting his arm around my shoulders. "And I'll bet you dance better than her right now."

Grinning with happiness, I slipped my arm around
Steve's waist and murmured, "Thanks."

We left the other guys and went into the parking lot.
"How about a walk on the beach?" Steve asked.

"Sure." I liked meeting Steve's friends, but I liked the
idea of being alone with him even more.

We strolled to the end of the street and started down the
beach to the ocean. The glow of the streetlights was soon
left behind and we continued on with only the light of the
half-moon to guide us. Steve held my hand and in a minute
we were at the water's edge, watching the dark waves lap
against the sand.

After the noise and excitement of The Club, the deserted beach was wonderfully quiet and peaceful. We took
off our sandals and walked hand in hand through the
shallow water. Neither of us spoke, but it didn't feel at all
strained or uncomfortable. It just seemed so right to be
there, walking together with the cool water at our feet and
the golden moon above our heads. Words weren't neces-
sary.

After a few minutes, Steve leaned over and picked
something up out of the water. He handed it to me and
when I held it up to the moonlight, I saw it was a small,

perfectly formed brown and white shell. I smiled and Steve said, "It's for you."

I opened my mouth to speak, but Steve leaned down to kiss me, a long, warm kiss that set my heart pounding. When it was over, Steve looked into my eyes and said, "Can you drive a car with a standard transmission?"

I burst out laughing, more from surprise than anything. "Yes," I said between giggles. "But why?"

Steve's expression was serious, except for the twinkle in his eye. "Because Land Rovers have standard transmissions and we'll have to buy one if we're going around the world. Some of the best surf is in the most remote places, you know."

I was still laughing, but inside I was amazed and thrilled. Was Steve serious? Did he really want me to come with him? I tried to imagine Steve and me, surfing our way around the world. It seemed like a fairy tale, a fantasy, a dream come true. But it could never be reality, could it? I mean, Steve had to go to California first, and I was still in high school. There was no way it could ever work out. No way.

That's what I told myself, but a little voice inside me whispered, "Why not?" and "It could happen," and finally, "Maybe."

Then Steve kissed me again, and anything seemed possible. His strong arms held me close and his lips were warm and soft against mine. I could hear the waves crashing against the sand and far in the distance, a buoy's bell clanged its warning into the night.

I don't know how long we stayed like that, but finally Steve whispered, "It's time for me to take you home."

Still carrying our sandals, we walked arm in arm up the beach to the street. Walking by the water, it had been easy to imagine we were the only two people in the world.

But no, there were still cars riding by, and people walking through the parking lot of The Club. Steve waved to someone he knew, but he kept his arm firmly around my waist. Then we got in the car and started up the boulevard toward Beach Haven.

Chapter Nine

When I woke up the next morning, I felt horrible. My head hurt and I was so tired I could barely open my eyes. I rolled over to go back to sleep, but then I remembered why I had to get up. Chris was coming in less than an hour!

I jumped up and quickly threw on some clothes. My hair didn't look terrific, but it would have to do. I brushed it out of my face, and hurried to the kitchen for breakfast. The house was empty and a note on the kitchen table told me the Bensons were at the beach. Tina had left a pot of coffee on the stove for me. Gratefully, I poured a cup and sat down at the table to think.

I tried to think about Chris. I told myself what a great guy he was and how much I missed him. That only worked about two minutes and then I was back to dreaming about Steve. In fact, that was the reason I was so exhausted. Steve had brought me home at one o'clock, but I spent the next two hours lying awake and thinking about him. I imagined us surfing around the world together, driving in our Land Rover and camping out on the beach. I imagined Steve winning the world championship surfing title and me being rated at the top of the women's division. I finally fell asleep and dreamed that the two of us were being interviewed on ABC's Wide World of Sports.

I made myself some toast and had another cup of coffee. My head still hurt so I took two aspirin. The next thing I knew, Chris was knocking at the door.

With a feeling of anticipation and dread, I opened the door and looked at Chris. The first thing I noticed was his height. After being around Steve, Chris seemed unusually tall and lanky. His curly brown hair was a little longer than usual and it looked good growing over his ears and on his forehead. I looked up into his face. It was as friendly and familiar as always, and when I smiled at Chris, he took me in his arms and hugged me.

"Oh, Kate," he whispered. "It's so good to see you." He kissed me and then hugged me again.

"Come on in," I told him. "Bill and Tina are at the beach with the kids. Do you want some coffee?"

"Sure." Chris was wearing jeans and a T-shirt that said TROWER PROFESSIONAL PAINTERS. He sat at the table and stretched out his long legs. It felt familiar and comfortable to be with him. Not exciting, like it was with Steve, but nice. I sat across from him and watched him sip his coffee.

"So," he said, "what have you been up to?"

Naturally, the first thing I thought of was Steve. It seemed a bit early to bring him up though, so I said, "Just taking care of Dee and Ricky and doing lots of surfing. Oh, and you'll never guess who's here for the summer. Cindy Levine! We've been hanging around together and you know what? I really like her."

We talked about Cindy awhile and I told Chris about seeing Jeep and The Spikes at The Club. Naturally, I didn't tell him I went there with Steve. Chris seemed pretty surprised that I was becoming friends with Cindy, but at least he didn't joke about her weird clothes or short hair, the way he usually did at school.

Just then I heard the front door open, and Dee and Ricky came running into the kitchen. I had told Bill and Tina that Chris was coming, but I hadn't mentioned it to the kids. I had this horrible fear that one of them might say something about Steve, but they didn't. They were too busy squealing with delight and jumping all over Chris. Then they had to tell him all about their morning at the beach and the big black dog they saw swimming.

Finally, Bill showed up to distract the kids and Tina came in to start lunch. "I want to take Kate out for lunch," Chris told her. "Where's a good place to go?"

"The Black Schooner is nice," suggested Tina. "It's right on the bay at Sixth Street."

"Okay," said Chris. "Let's go. And bring your bathing suit so we can go swimming afterward."

We got into Chris's old gray Buick and started off down the boulevard. It wasn't as much fun as being in Steve's white Mustang with the top down and the radio playing. The radio in Chris's car didn't even work.

At The Black Schooner we got a table on the patio overlooking the bay. Seagulls circled above us, squawking and diving for food. We both ordered lobster salad sandwiches and Chris said, "Kate, I have some good news. I talked to Coach Oakley and he told me Penn is sending a scout to take a look at me next season."

Chris had always wanted to go to the University of Pennsylvania. His dad had gone there and so had his uncle. Chris was hoping to get a basketball scholarship and then study political science and law. We had often talked about going there together. I'd always liked the idea of going to college in the city and of being there with Chris.

Now I wasn't so sure. Steve's dream of surfing around

the world had really sparked my imagination. Sure, it was less safe and predictable than going to Penn and majoring in phys. ed. or English, but it sounded an awful lot more fun. I loved surfing and I had always wanted to travel. And with Steve there beside me, I just knew it would be great.

"That's wonderful," I told Chris, but I knew I didn't sound very enthusiastic.

"What's wrong?" he asked.

"Nothing. It *is* wonderful for you. I just don't know if I want to go to Penn too. I don't know if I want to go to any college right away."

Chris reached out and took my hand. "I never heard you say that before," he said seriously. "What made you change your mind?"

Now was the time to tell him about Steve. I opened my mouth, but nothing came out. Chris looked so worried, so concerned. I just couldn't bring myself to hurt him. Besides, how could I break the news in the middle of lunch? We'd probably both get sick to our stomachs.

"I don't know," I said casually. "It's nothing serious." I smiled and said, "Tell me about the gang. How are Rachel and Amy doing?"

Listening to Chris talk about our friends at home, I started to relax and enjoy myself. Fairbanks was something we both shared, something we both cared about. Chris told me that Amy had broken up with her college boyfriend and Rachel almost lost her job at McDonald's when she dropped an entire tray of hamburgers on the floor. He told me about last weekend, when the gang went up to the lake and Shawn Faber got a ticket for doing three miles over the speed limit. We talked about the new record store that was opening downtown and about the prospects of the basketball and swim teams next year.

By the time we left the restaurant, I was feeling pretty good. After all, I liked Chris. If I didn't, I wouldn't have gone steady with him for two years. We had our own private jokes and special ways of doing things and we enjoyed each other's company. I felt relaxed when I was with him, the same way I did with my female friends or with my brother, John.

After lunch, Chris drove to the beach. We were both wearing our bathing suits under our clothes so when we got to the parking lot, we took off our jeans and T-shirts in the car. The beach was crowded, so we ended up far from the water, near the dunes. We spread out our towels and sat down.

It seemed strange to be at the beach without Steve. Whenever I was with him, we either surfed or talked about surfing. Chris, of course, was different. He had no interest in how big the waves were or how they were breaking. He just wanted to throw his frisbee around and splash through the surf.

At first I tried to talk to Chris about surfing. He listened for a few minutes but soon got bored and started talking about his summer job. That really annoyed me, especially since I had spent at least three lifetimes listening to Chris talk about basketball. After a while though, I forgot about surfing and got into swapping summer-job stories with Chris. Chris is a good storyteller and he always knows how to make me laugh.

"There we were," Chris was saying, "working on the eighth floor. Ted was stirring the paint and I was scraping the old paint off the wood. Then I happened to glance in the nearest window and I almost fell off the scaffold. There was a woman in there, wearing nothing but a towel. She was looking right at me and when she knew I'd seen her, she started to drop the towel! I jumped back and knocked the paint can right off the scaffold. We spent the rest of the afternoon cleaning it up!''

We both laughed and Chris reached out and took my hand. "She wasn't as pretty as you," he said softly. He leaned closer and kissed me, a warm, friendly kiss just like so many he had given me before. It didn't make my heart pound like it did when Steve kissed me, but it felt good.

"Even if we're not together this summer," Chris said, "you're still my girl." He smiled and added, "Nothing changes that."

Now was the moment to tell Chris about Steve. It wasn't fair to let him think I was his girl, when I was really spending all my time with someone else. But how could I? Chris was being so nice to me. I knew it wasn't easy for him to accept the fact that I had picked a summer at the shore over a summer with him. How could I tell him I'd chosen a new boyfriend too?

Besides, I told myself, I still didn't know how Steve really felt about me. I knew he liked me, but how much? For all I knew, he might be dating other girls besides me. He might even be seeing his old girlfriend, Lisa.

And what about our dream of surfing around the world together? I knew Steve was serious about going, but was he also serious about taking me? I had no way of knowing. Maybe when Steve went off to California and I went back to Fairbanks, he would forget all about me. There were probably lots of girls in California who surfed. He'd be sure to fall for one of them, and then I'd be stuck at Fairbanks High School with no boyfriend and no date for the senior prom.

I leaned over and kissed the freckle on Chris's ear. "I'm glad you came to visit me," I said. Well, at least I wasn't lying. It's true I hadn't been looking forward to seeing Chris, but now that he was here, I was glad.

"Hey," Chris said, "I have an idea. Let's get your board and go surfing. With your expert instructions, I should be able to get the hang of it."

"No!" I said, a little too loudly. There was no way I was going to take Chris surfing. What if we ran into Steve or one of his friends? "The beaches are too crowded in the afternoon," I lied. "Besides, I get to surf every day. I'd rather do something else with you."

Fortunately, Chris agreed. I don't think he really wanted to go surfing. He just suggested it because he thought it would please me. We finally decided on a movie in Surf City, a new comedy we both wanted to see.

After the movie, Chris drove me home. "I better be heading back," he said. "I have to start work at seven o'clock tomorrow."

"Boy, your dad sounds like a slave driver." I laughed. "Doesn't he know the boss's son is supposed to get all the breaks?"

"Not my dad. He thinks I have to work twice as hard to prove myself." Chris shrugged his shoulders. "I don't really mind though. I'm saving a lot of money for college. If this basketball scholarship doesn't come through, I'm going to need it."

I had to admire Chris's determination and good sense. He knew just what he wanted and how to get it. I, on the other hand, had no idea what I wanted to do after high school. Secretly, I always dreamed of doing something wild and exciting, something really different, but what that something would be, I didn't know. I guess I figured it would just come to me one day, and suddenly I would take off on some wild adventure. In the meantime, I acted like everyone else. I went to high school, worked hard to get into Penn with Chris, and waited for inspiration.

Maybe that's why I liked Steve so much. He had a plan, but it wasn't a safe, secure one like Chris's. His goal was unique and exciting, just the sort of thing I had always dreamed of. Could it be that surfing around the world was what I wanted too? Was that the wild, exciting something I'd been waiting for? I wasn't sure, but I knew I was ready to find out.

"Kate? Kate!" Chris was shaking my shoulder. "You're a million miles away. What in the world are you thinking about?"

"Just surfing," I answered vaguely. "I'm sorry." Chris put his arm around me and suddenly I remembered the black T-shirt I had bought for him at Bay Village. It was in the bottom drawer of my bureau, next to Chris's letter. "Wait here," I told him. "I have a present for you."

I ran into the house and returned with the T-shirt. "Hey, this is great!" exclaimed Chris. "Thanks, Kate." He pulled off his old T-shirt and put it on. As I had predicted, the shirt looked good on Chris, especially the stars that sparkled across his slender chest.

Chris put his arms around my waist and kissed me. "So long, Kate," he said. "I'll be thinking about you. And I'll be back again as soon as I can."

" 'Bye, Chris," I said warmly, giving him an enthusiastic hug. Now that Chris was leaving, I wanted him to stay. I liked him. Besides, having him around made me feel secure. I knew he loved me and that felt good.

Chris hopped in his car and backed down the driveway. "Write to me!" he called. I waved, Chris honked his horn, and then he was gone.

I stopped waving and stood in the empty driveway with my arms hanging down at my sides. Despite the fun I'd had with Chris, I felt guilty and miserable. I had started the day with every intention of settling things, and look what happened. I hadn't broken up with Chris. I hadn't even wanted to. With a sigh, I turned and walked back to the house. Boy, was I confused!

Chapter Ten

I guess there's some truth to that old saying, "Out of sight, out of mind." At first I couldn't stop thinking about Chris. All through Sunday evening I wondered, do I love him or don't I? Do I want to break up with him? Should I tell him about Steve? The questions went round and round in my head until I thought I'd never fall asleep. But by the next day, I had almost forgotten about Chris. That sounds rotten, I know, but really, I was so busy, I didn't have time to think about anything that wasn't right in front of me. There was just too much going on.

On Monday I took Dee and Ricky to the bird sanctuary at the southern tip of the Island. It was pretty hard to keep the kids quiet, so naturally we didn't see too many birds. There were sea gulls though, and lots of sandpipers.

Ricky was wild about the sandpipers. He loved the way they could run right down to the water's edge and then scuttle back before the waves covered their feet.

"Look at me, Kate!" he cried. "I'm a sandpiper!" He hopped down to the water and then jumped back before the wave swept over his toes.

Naturally, Dee wanted to show off too. She skipped down to join Ricky, while I sat near the dunes and

watched. Their game soon changed, however, and instead
of avoiding the waves, they were hopping into them,
leaping into the air and landing with a splash.

It wasn't until I noticed how wet the kids were getting
that I realized what was going on. Dee actually had her
feet in the water! True, she wasn't swimming or anything,
but it was the closest she'd gotten to water since she fell in
the YMCA pool. I could hardly wait to tell Bill and Tina.
This was a real breakthrough!

A few minutes later, the kids ran back to me, carrying a
dead starfish they had found in the sand. "A star!" announced Ricky triumphantly.

"No, dummy, a starfish," Dee corrected him. "His
name is Moe."

We put Moe in my knapsack and continued walking
down the beach. I waited until Ricky was occupied,
throwing a piece of driftwood and chasing it. Then I asked
Dee, "Would you like to see me surf someday? Without
Ricky," I added.

Dee looked interested. "Yes, take me."

"Okay. We can go with Cindy. You can help me wax
my board."

Dee nodded, and I felt good. If Dee got really excited
about surfing, she might agree to come into the water with
me. Even if she didn't want to jump right in, she might at
least let me push her around on my board. Once she was
actually out there with me, I was pretty sure her fear of
water would vanish. Anyway, it was worth a try.

The next morning, I got a postcard from Chris. The
photo on the front was of the Fairbanks firehouse and
above it, Chris had scribbled, "Another quality job by
Trower Professional Painters!" I turned the card over.
"Dear Kate," it said. "It was great to see you. The gang

loves my T-shirt. Everyone promises to write (but don't hold your breath). I hope to be back to see you in two or three weeks. I miss you already. Love, Chris.''

I threw the postcard in my bottom drawer, next to the other letter from Chris. I felt miserable. Why hadn't I broken up with Chris the way I'd planned. In a week or two he'd be back and I'd have to go through the whole thing again, including lying to Steve.

All right, I told myself firmly. So he'll be back. This time you can tell him the truth and then you won't have to lie anymore. But who was to say I'd do any better next time? Breaking up with Chris sounded good in theory, but when we were face to face, I just couldn't go through with it. There was something about that kind face and those trusting gray eyes that just seemed to melt my resolve.

That afternoon I curled up on my bed with one of Tina's notecards, a new felt-tipped pen and an envelope addressed to Chris. I knew it was the coward's way out, but how else could I break up with him? At least this way he wouldn't drive down to visit and I could keep my Sundays open in case Steve wanted to go on another picnic.

I'd gotten as far as the ''Dear Chris'' part when the phone rang. Gratefully, I ran to the kitchen and answered it.

''Hey, Kate! This is Steve.''

Instantly, I put the letter to Chris out of my mind. ''Hi,'' I said happily. ''How are you?''

''Good. It's too bad you couldn't come surfing on Sunday. The waves were good and there were a couple of photographers on the beach. Last time they were around, a picture of me showed up in *Surfer*.''

''It was pretty boring here,'' I lied. ''I took Dee and Ricky to the beach and out for pizza.''

''Well, here's something to cheer you up. Meet me at

The Curl in half an hour. It's about time you turned in that rental board and got one of your own.''

Thirty minutes later I was standing outside The Curl with my rented surfboard. Steve soon appeared and I watched as he parked his car and walked across the street. As he came closer, I felt my heartbeat quicken and my knees turn to rubber. Steve was so handsome! The white bathing suit and white T-shirt he wore made his skin look almost bronze. His legs and arms were muscular and his shoulders were broad. When he saw me, his face broke into a grin and he ran a hand through his silky blond hair. It felt wonderful knowing he was walking to meet me.

"Hi, Kate." Steve kissed me lightly and took my hand. "You look terrific."

I could feel my face glowing with happiness as we walked into The Curl. My spirits fell, however, when I saw the salesman who had rented me my surfboard. Would he remember my dumb remark about the Matt Kechele poster?

"Hey, Mack, how's it going?" said Steve. "I'm going to show Kate some boards." Steve turned to me and added, "Mack is my boss, you know. A nice guy, but since he got that surfboard in the head in '62, he's never been the same."

At first I wasn't sure if Steve was serious. Mack looked like a pretty weird guy. He was almost old enough to be my father, but he had shoulder-length hair and a bushy gray beard. His teeth were gnarled and one of the front ones was missing. I could almost believe that he'd been hit by a surfboard one too many times.

But when both Steve and Mack burst out laughing, I relaxed. "Don't let Steve sell you a used board," Mack said, leaning over the counter and winking at me. "It might be one he worked on, and in that case it's sure to snap in two on your first time out.''

I giggled and Mack went back to reading a surfing magazine. "Come on," said Steve. "I'll show you where I work.''

I followed Steve into the back room. It was a small space, crowded with sawhorses, tools and surfboards in various states of disrepair. The floor was littered with empty paper cups, soda cans and cigarette butts. An open door let in air and sunlight and next to it stood one of the boys Steve had introduced me to at The Club.

"Hey, T.J.," said Steve. "Working hard?''

T.J. was small and muscular, with wavy black hair and a mustache. He wore only a bathing suit and sneakers and he was drinking orange juice straight from the carton. "Oh, sure," he said. "Hi," he added, smiling at me.

"Remember Kate?" Steve asked. "We're looking at the boards today.''

"Yeah," nodded T.J. He took a gulp of orange juice. "Hey, when are we going to see you surf, Kate? Steve says you're getting good.''

I grinned nervously. Had Steve really been talking about me? "You'll see her soon," Steve answered, putting his arm around me. "So far we've been sticking to the most deserted beaches." He looked at me and added, "I've been keeping Kate all to myself.''

I was smiling with pleasure as Steve waved to T.J. and led me back to the front of the shop. We stopped in front of a row of surfboards and Steve said, "Do you want to look around?''

There were at least fifty boards against the wall and more outside. "I don't know where to begin," I answered. "Don't you have any suggestions?''

Steve grinned. "I thought you'd never ask." He pointed to a small blue twin-fin. "This is your best buy. It's great in small surf. Very maneuverable and versatile. Perfect for beginners." Steve went on to explain a lot of technical things about how the board was made, but I was already sold. Steve knew surfboards, and besides, the price was right. With the discount Steve would get, I could just afford it. I'd even have five or six dollars left until payday!'

Since I was a friend of Steve's, Mack let me write a check. "Surf well on it," he said, lifting the board off the wall rack.

"You carry it out," said Steve. "I'll be right there."

Proudly, I carried my new board to the Mustang. It looked great sticking out of the back seat next to Steve's red and black board. I ran my hand over the smooth blue fins and whispered, "My very own surfboard!" And maybe someday it would be tied to the top of a Land Rover while Steve and I drove through some remote section of Australia or South America, searching for the perfect wave.

I saw Steve emerge from The Curl and jog toward me. Before he got in the car, he tossed me a cardboard mailing tube. "The Matt Kechele poster," he said teasingly. "Or is it Mark Richards?" I laughed and Steve said, "Anyway, I thought you'd like to have it."

Steve and I spent the rest of the afternoon surfing. My new board was terrific—light, fast, and easy to handle— and I found myself making turns I'd never been able to bring off before. Steve was really impressed. "That clinches it," he said, as we straddled our boards, waiting for the next set of waves. "You *have* to enter the Championships now. You're really good."

"Oh, come on Steve," I countered. "There'll be surfers there from all over the East Coast. I can't stand up to that kind of competition.''

"Why not?" he asked. "Besides, it doesn't matter if you win or not. You must know from your swimming experience that just about no one wins his first competition. What you gain is the experience to go on to the next contest and the next, until you do win. And that feels good.''

"I know." I was thinking about all the swim meets I'd competed in. When I'd first tried out for the team at the beginning of freshman year, I barely made it. The coach told me later the only reason he didn't cut me was because I had a swimmer's body and a good attitude and he figured I might develop into a decent swimmer. He was right, because by the end of last year, I was the best girl on the team, and I loved to compete. It's funny because I'd never been all that competitive in other things. I'm usually pretty easygoing and relaxed. But there's something about swimming in a race that really excites me. I wondered if surfing in the Long Beach Island Surf Championships would make me feel the same way.

"Kate." I looked up. Steve's expression was serious. "I don't want to push you into anything," he said. "Just because I'm so intense about surfing doesn't mean you have to be. You enjoy surfing and I want it to stay that way. Don't feel you have to compete just because I'm suggesting it.''

I thought about what Steve was saying. He was right, of course. There was no reason why I had to compete. Still, the more I thought about it, the more the idea appealed to me. Surfing excited me in a way nothing else ever had. It was like swimming, but even better because you weren't just going back and forth across a pool, endlessly repeating the same moves. In surfing, you were competing against the wave and against yourself. One mistake and the wave got you, throwing you off your board and choking you in the foam. But if you could ride the wave and tame it, there was no end to what you could do—tricks and turns that sent you shooting across the wave or practically flying into the air. Nope, there was no doubt about it. I was as excited about surfing as Steve was. It was the best feeling in the world.

I looked at Steve and nodded. "I'm going to enter," I told him.

"Kate, are you . . ."

"I'm sure," I said. "Absolutely."

Steve looked into my eyes and nodded. "I know that look," he said. "Surf fever!"

As the next wave appeared we both started paddling and took off side by side. I glanced at Steve. He looked so handsome and graceful crouching over his board as it shot across the long, green wave. I dropped to one knee and followed close behind. "Go for it!" Steve yelled. I laughed and tasted salt water on my tongue. I felt terrific!

Chapter Eleven

I never wrote that letter to Chris. Instead, I took out a new
envelope and used the notecard to write to my parents. I
told them about Cindy, about Dee and Ricky at the bird
sanctuary, and about my new surfboard, but I didn't
mention anything about Steve. I told myself it would be
better to wait until I broke up with Chris and everything
was settled. Deep down inside, I think I knew I wasn't
handling things very well, and I didn't want my parents to
find out. Meanwhile, I promised myself I'd explain things
to Chris the next time he drove down to visit. I couldn't do
anything until then, so I just put him out of my mind.

With Chris out of the picture, I was able to really enjoy
myself. Cindy and I were getting to be good friends. She
spent a couple mornings a week with the kids and me, and
I came to visit her at the bakery at night. We ate so many
cookies and doughnuts that one day Cindy announced she
had gained ten pounds. I probably would have too, if it
wasn't for all the surfing I was doing. After that, we
switched to diet soda and fruit, and Cindy started losing
weight.

Cindy had a portable tape deck that she usually brought

along to the beach. She had tapes of all kinds of rock music and she seemed to know something about every group. I'd never listened to anything but the Top 40, so most of the songs were new to me. I liked a lot of it, and Cindy made longer tapes of my favorite groups. She also had a tape of The Spikes and after I'd heard it a few times, their songs didn't sound all the same anymore. Cindy knew all the words and pretty soon I did too. We liked to sing along, either seriously or in silly voices when we wanted to crack each other up.

While Cindy was teaching me about rock music, I was introducing her to fantasy novels. I lent her *The Snow Queen* and bought her the first book of the *Narnia Chronicles*. She loved it and picked up the rest of the series herself. We went to movies too, including a kiddie matinee of *Fantasia*. We had a great time oohing and aahing along with all the ten-year-olds.

One Monday evening Cindy took me over to her house to look at her art. Jeep was out practicing with The Spikes and his parents were visiting friends so we had the house to ourselves. Usually Cindy seemed extremely self-confident—almost cocky—but as soon as we got in the house she became quiet and nervous.

"Sit down," she said softly. "Do you want something to drink?"

"Show me your artwork first," I replied.

Cindy looked at her feet. "All right." She left me in the living room and while I waited, I looked around. The house was a modern A-frame, filled with Scandinavian design furniture and dramatic black-and-white photographs. On the coffee table there was a picture of Jeep as a baby. He was bald and pudgy and wore a sailor suit. I could just imagine how much Jeep must hate that photo now!

Finally, Cindy returned carrying a large art portfolio. She placed it on my lap and said, "I can't bear to watch while anyone looks at my work." And softer, "Especially someone I care about." She turned quickly. "I'll go make some iced tea."

Eagerly, I opened the portfolio. Cindy's art was really amazing! There were a dozen charcoal portraits, including a self-portrait, and the rest of the portfolio was filled with photographs of Cindy's sculpture. Some of it was beautiful and some of it was funny (like a strange wall hanging made out of dental floss and toothbrushes) but all of it was eye-catching and unique.

"I love this!" I exclaimed.

Sheepishly, Cindy stuck her head around the corner. "You do?"

"Yes." She looked dubious. "Yes, yes, yes!" I shouted.

Cindy's face lit up. "Then come out on the deck. I'll show you what I'm working on now."

I followed Cindy through the kitchen and on to a porch that faced the ocean. When we got outside, she flipped on the light. "Wow!" I gasped. Half the porch was taken up with a huge sculpture made entirely from old car parts. Some of them I recognized—headlights, a couple of mufflers and an entire door—but most of it I couldn't identify. The sculpture had a vaguely human shape, making it look like a giant space creature. Cindy plugged in an extension cord. The headlights turned on and a fan began to turn.

I laughed. "This is great! It looks like an extraterrestrial."

"It is." She giggled. "From the planet Chevrolet."

Cindy seemed much more comfortable now. She didn't say anything, but I think she'd been really worried I wouldn't like her sculpture. It was crazy, I couldn't deny that, but I really did like it. Still laughing, we turned off the lights and went inside for some iced tea.

When I wasn't taking care of Dee and Ricky or hanging out with Cindy, I was surfing with Steve. We spent every afternoon together, usually at the popular beaches at the southern end of the Island. Steve liked to be where everybody knew him, and I couldn't blame him. All his friends were there, as well as a lot of awe-struck young surfers who just stood around and watched him. When photographers showed up, they always aimed their cameras at Steve. That meant publicity, an important consideration if Steve was going to turn professional.

For the most part, I enjoyed Steve's popularity. I liked getting to know his friends, and I enjoyed being with someone who was always the center of attention. I was proud of Steve and wanted everyone to like him.

The only thing I didn't like was the girls. There were lots of them on the beach, either friends of the other surfers or girls who just came by to check out the boys. All of them seemed interested in Steve. They watched him as he carried his board in and out of the water and jumped at any chance to start a conversation with him. Steve never paid much attention, but I couldn't help feeling he enjoyed being chased by all those girls. When they were watching him, he walked across the beach a little slower and his surfing was even more exciting and daring than usual.

I really wouldn't have minded if I'd been sure of Steve's feelings for me. Oh, I knew he liked me. After all, we spent almost every afternoon together, and we had gone on a couple more Sunday picnics. But I really couldn't tell how serious he was about me. Even though we still talked about surfing around the world together, we never planned anything or made any promises. It was all just a fantasy, an enjoyable way to pass the time. And even though Steve introduced me to all his friends, he never called me his girlfriend. For all I know, I could have been nothing more than "a nice girl who surfs" to him.

Much as I wanted to know if Steve was really serious about me, I never felt I could ask. The reason, of course, was Chris. During the next few weeks he came to visit two more times, and on both occasions I was totally unable to break up with him. Both visits were the same. I started out determined to bring everything out in the open, but when I saw Chris's familiar face, my resolve crumbled. I still spent a good part of each visit silently comparing him to Steve (with Chris usually losing out) but even that didn't matter. I told myself I really liked Chris and enjoyed being with him, but I knew I had another reason for not breaking up with him. Although I was confident Steve liked me, I knew Chris *loved* me, and that was something I just couldn't bear to give up.

Then one day, things changed. The afternoon started normally enough. Steve picked me up after work and we drove to our favorite beach. Mark and T.J. were both there and we all paddled out together. We'd been out about a half hour when we noticed four or five guys near the water's edge, waxing down their boards.

"I never saw them before," remarked T.J. "Do you know them, Steve?"

"Nope. Probably summer kids who just showed up."

"Or guys from Cape May or Ocean City," suggested Mark.

The unknown surfers were soon forgotten as a new set of waves began. Steve, Mark and T.J. took off on the first three, but I held back, waiting for a larger wave to try out some turns I was working on. As I waited, the new guys threw their boards in the water and paddled out.

"Hi!" said one, a cute blond with dimples.

"Hi," I replied, turning around to watch the waves forming behind me.

"How's the surf today?" asked another.

I turned back, and noticed that all five guys had paddled up next to me. They weren't even in position to catch a wave. They were just looking at me and smiling. "Uh, pretty good," I answered self-consciously. "It was bigger last week."

The conversation continued like that, with the guys asking me lots of questions about Long Beach Island and surfing in general. They seemed extremely interested in everything I had to say. At first I couldn't figure out why they picked me to talk to. There were at least ten other surfers in the water, including Steve, who was obviously the best surfer on the beach. But I soon decided I didn't care. I was enjoying myself. I liked being the center of attention, especially when my admirers were good-looking boys.

"We're from Massachusetts," the boy with dimples told me. "Cape Cod." He grinned and added, "We never see any female surfers up there."

"Yeah," agreed another, a boy with shoulder-length hair and a gold chain around his neck. "Especially not beautiful ones."

I laughed and said, "Oh, sure." I figured they were just teasing, but they kept on complimenting me.

"You're a good surfer," said one. "You pulled off an amazing backside layback on that last wave."

I was going to say that Steve was really the best at hot dog surfing. All the tricks I knew, I'd learned from him. But I didn't say it. At that moment I didn't know where Steve was and I didn't care. For once I wasn't surfing in

Steve's shadow and I wasn't sitting there watching while a bunch of pretty girls talked to him. This time, I was the one who was being admired, and I loved it.

I was just about to explain how I pulled off the backside layback, when someone said, "Are you guys surfing, or just taking up room out here?"

We all turned around. It was Steve with Mark and T.J. behind him. "We're just talking," replied the boy with the gold chain.

"Yeah," said another, "and taking in the scenery."

Steve paddled closer. "Well, why don't you get into nature at some other beach?" he said angrily. "Kate's not some beach bunny put here for you to drool over."

"Who are you, her brother?" asked the blond boy testily.

Steve's voice was dangerously calm. "No," he said, carefully enunciating each word. "I'm her boyfriend. So just take off."

"Is that right?" replied one of the boys. "Well, why don't we hear what *she* has to say about it?"

They all turned and looked at me, but I barely noticed. I was looking at Steve and feeling terrific. He had said he was my boyfriend, right in front of everybody.

"I'm Steve's girlfriend," I said firmly. I paddled over beside him.

"Well, *excuse us*," said the dimpled boy with fake concern. His friends laughed.

"This is a lousy beach anyway," added the boy with the gold chain. "Let's go." They all paddled toward shore and Steve and I turned to face each other. Mark and T.J. paddled away from us and caught the next wave in.

Steve was silent for a minute. Then he said softly, "Did you just do that to make me jealous?"

"No, of course not," I answered quickly. "They just

started talking to me. That's all.''

"But you were loving it, I could tell." Steve sounded really hurt. "I saw the way you were looking at them."

"Well, Steve," I said, my voice rising, "it's no different than the way you act when all the girls around here talk to you. Besides, how was I supposed to know you cared? You never told anyone before that you were my boyfriend. Most of the time you just treat me like one of the guys."

I stopped talking and looked down at my board. Fearfully, I waited for Steve to reply. I wanted so much for him to say he loved me, to tell me he could never see me as just one of the guys. But would he? Maybe my angry outburst had made him angry too. Maybe he would just paddle away and leave me. I wanted to know how Steve felt about me, but I was frightened of being hurt.

Steve was staring straight ahead of him. Slowly, he turned and looked into my eyes. "Kate," he said, "I'm sorry. I guess I never realized until now just how much I care for you." He paused and then said, "Listen Kate, breaking up with Lisa was painful. That's why after it was over, I decided I didn't want to get serious about anyone for a while. When I met you, I just wanted to have fun. Nothing too heavy, especially since you had to go back to high school in the fall. But it hasn't worked. I love you, Kate. More than I loved Lisa. More than I ever loved anyone." He frowned and asked, "Do you understand?"

I could hardly speak. My heart was so filled with love for Steve, I thought it would burst out of my chest. "Yes," I whispered. "And Steve, I love you too."

Steve tried to hug me, but with each of us straddling a surfboard, it was almost impossible. Laughing, Steve jumped into the water and pulled himself on to my board so we were sitting face to face. All the other surfers were staring at us, I knew, but I didn't care. Still laughing, we hugged each other. Then Steve kissed me and I could taste the salt water on his lips and feel his cool wet hair against my face. It was the most wonderful feeling in the world.

Chapter Twelve

After Steve said he loved me, I made a solemn promise to myself. The next time Chris came to visit, I would tell him everything. I would explain about Steve, I'd apologize for lying to him, and I would thank him for all the love he'd given me and all the good times we'd had together. Then I'd break up with him—finally, definitely and forever.

But Chris didn't come. He wrote me a letter saying he was working overtime for his father and spending all his spare time playing basketball at the YMCA. Saving money for college and preparing for the upcoming basketball season had to be his prime concerns, he explained, even though he hated not being able to spend time with me. He ended by promising to visit as soon as he possibly could.

Chris's letter was a relief. I knew I had to break up with him, but it wasn't something I was looking forward to. Any chance to postpone things was all right with me. Gratefully, I put Chris out of my mind and concentrated on Steve.

The time I spent with Steve was wonderful. We surfed

every afternoon and all day Sunday. Steve was coaching me for the Championships and my surfing was really improving. On weekend evenings, we went to The Club to dance and hang out with our friends. Then we would walk on the beach, kiss, and weave our dreams about surfing around the world.

There was only one thing wrong. When I first met Steve he had told me of his plan to go to California in September. He wanted to surf the big waves of the West Coast and Hawaii and enter the important competitions that would pave the way for him to turn pro. His parents, he'd told me, were against the idea. They wanted him to go to college in New Jersey and do his surfing around here.

After our first few meetings, Steve hadn't mentioned California again. I assumed his parents had vetoed the idea and Steve was resigned to staying in New Jersey, at least for a while. That was fine with me. The thought of Steve moving away in September was so upsetting, I didn't even want to think about it. Instead, I fantasized about how much fun it would be having a college boyfriend during my senior year at Fairbanks. We could see each other every weekend and Steve would invite me to dances and football games at his school. And of course he would be my date for the senior prom. I couldn't wait to show him off to Rachel and Amy.

But all my fantasies began to crumble when Steve started talking about California again. His parents were still against it, but he had a plan. A cousin who lived near Huntington Beach was trying to find Steve a job. If he had a place to stay and a way to support himself, Steve figured there was no way his parents could say no.

After I met Steve's parents though, I wasn't so sure. They wanted to meet Steve's new girlfriend, so he invited me for dinner one evening. We ate fresh swordfish and talked about the changes that had taken place on Long Beach Island since the Mathesons had opened their marina in 1953. They were nice, but pretty conservative, and it was clear that they were dead set against Steve's plans. As far as I could tell, Mr. Matheson wanted Steve to study business at Ocean County College and help him run the marina. He didn't like the idea of Steve becoming a professional surfer at all.

When Steve drove me home that night, I tried to put in a few good words for staying in New Jersey. I didn't want to push it though. For one thing, I was afraid Steve would get angry. I remembered what he had told me about his old girlfriend, Lisa. "She didn't understand about surfing," he'd said. "She thought it was something for kids, something I would outgrow." I certainly didn't want him to think I felt like that!

Besides, I knew Steve was right. If he was going to become famous, he had to make his mark on the West Coast as well as the East. All I could do was wait, and see what Steve decided. In the meantime, I took my usual action when faced with something unpleasant. I decided not to think about it.

The summer was passing much too quickly. It was almost August already, and in four weeks I'd be surfing in the Long Beach Island Championships. Steve and I filled out registration blanks at The Curl and were given a sheet of contest rules and regulations. The next week Steve drove down to Florida and placed second in the East Coast Surf Classic. He returned home determined to take a first in the L.B.I. Championships.

Steve's enthusiasm was catching. Where I had once been horrified at the thought of even entering the contest, I now fantasized about placing in the top ten. We surfed every day until sunset, practicing and refining our moves.

On the first Saturday of August, the weather service predicted severe rains with high winds and lightning. Storm warnings were in effect and small craft were advised to keep off the water until further notice. I resigned myself to spending a few days in the house, and of course, no surfing.

Sunday morning was cloudy and humid. It wasn't raining yet, but black clouds huddled on the horizon and a strong wind blew sand into the streets. The Bensons were going out to brunch with friends from the mainland. After they left, the house was dark and silent. I made tea and sat in the living room, scaring myself with a Stephen King novel.

Steve and I had planned to spend the day together, surfing and swimming. I wondered if he would call with an alternative plan or just show up. Maybe we'd go to a movie or just hang around the house and watch TV.

When I heard Steve's car pull into the driveway, I ran out on to the porch. Steve had put up the top on the Mustang, but I was surprised to see he'd brought his surfboard. It was sticking out of the trunk and the door was held down with rope.

Steve stuck his head out of the window. His eyes were wide with excitement and he was grinning as he said, "Hurry up, Kate. Get in."

"Where are we going?" I asked, walking toward the car.

"Surfing, of course. Come on."

I stopped. "Are you kidding? It's going to rain any minute."

Steve was almost jumping up and down in the seat. "I

know!'' he said. ''The waves are huge. Just incredible! I can't wait to get out there.''

''But, Steve, it's dangerous!'' I was worried now. Worried and scared. Everyone knows you're not supposed to go in the water when it's raining, especially not in a huge storm like the one that would soon hit Long Beach Island. You could get hit by lightning. You could be killed.

Steve stopped grinning. ''Okay, okay,'' he said seriously. ''Listen, I don't want *you* to go out, Kate. In fact, I guess I shouldn't even have come over. But the waves are amazing. Even if it is dangerous, I've just got to go out. I've got to!''

I looked into Steve's determined blue eyes and I knew he was going surfing—with or without me. To Steve, those big waves were both a threat and a challenge. It was like they were daring him to surf, daring him to prove he could do it. He just couldn't say no.

I was still looking at Steve. ''There's nothing I can do to stop you, is there?''

Steve smiled with one side of his mouth. ''No, little kitten. No way.''

''Then I'm going with you.'' I ran and opened the door before Steve could change his mind. ''Let's go,'' I said firmly and we took off down the boulevard toward Holgate.

The sky was like a gray blanket, hanging low over our heads. The wind was blowing sand everywhere. There aren't many trees on Long Beach Island, but even the bushes were bent over and a shutter was flapping wildly on one of the houses we passed. There were only a few cars on the street, and no one was walking.

Steve didn't say a word during the ride and I was pretty

sure it was because of me. He had come over to share something exciting with me, and all I'd done was react like a frightened school girl. No wonder Steve was bummed out. I'd acted like a real party pooper.

Don't worry so much Kate, I told myself. Steve is a fabulous surfer. He'll be fine. Just fine. But I couldn't calm down. What if the rough surf was too much for Steve? I'm a good swimmer, but I wasn't sure I could rescue him in choppy water. And what if a bolt of lightning hit Steve while he was surfing? I didn't even want to think about that.

Steve pulled into the parking lot next to our favorite beach. There were no other cars and no one else in sight. The air was filled with so much sand, I could barely see the water. Steve grabbed a wet-suit vest from the back seat and put it on. I hoped that would be enough to keep him warm. As for me, I was wearing only jeans and a sweat shirt. I hadn't even thought to bring a jacket. The temperature was dropping rapidly and I was starting to shiver.

Steve looked at me and smiled grimly. "Here I go," he said. He hopped out and pulled his board from the trunk. When I got out too he said, "Maybe you should stay here, Kate."

"No way," I answered. "I want to keep an eye on you." I held Steve's arm. "And you watch me too. If it starts to rain, I'll wave you in, okay?"

"Aw, Kate, I—"

"Promise me," I insisted. "If I wave to you, you'll come right in."

Steve frowned. "Okay." He hugged his board impatiently. "Come on. Let's go."

Together, Steve and I made our way down the beach. The sand was blowing so hard, we had to shield our eyes.

It wasn't until we were almost at the water's edge that I could see the surf clearly.

"Wow!" I gasped. Now I understood why Steve was so excited. The waves were huge! They were also rough and powerful. They broke unexpectedly and often, spraying up mountains of foam as they crashed. I was frightened just looking at them. Frightened and exhilarated.

Steve must have felt the same way. He was breathing quickly and practically hopping up and down. "Now," he was muttering. "Now." Was he trying to convince himself to paddle out? Was he really going to do it?

"Now!" Without looking back, Steve threw his board into the water and started paddling. Almost immediately I lost sight of him. Then he appeared again, a bit of color amid the choppy gray surf. When I caught sight of him again, he was straddling his board, ready to take off.

I looked at the sky. It was turning from gray to black, but there was still no thunder and lightning and no rain. Quickly, I looked back at Steve just in time to see him take off on an enormous wave. Horrified, I held my breath. Steve slid straight down the wave and cut back just in time to keep from wiping out. He turned left, but almost immediately the wave began to collapse and he had to cut right. Shooting up the rim, he stayed on for another few yards before the wave closed in on him and he had to bail out.

As soon as possible, Steve was up again. With each wave, he seemed to gain more control, until soon he was hot dogging through the choppy surf, taking incredible risks and making unbelievable moves. In fact, he was doing tricks I'd never seen before. And through it all, he hardly ever wiped out.

Meanwhile, I stood on the shore trying to sort out my

emotions. The most obvious one was fear. Steve was continually on the verge of wiping out. Usually he cut back at the last second, saving himself from the crashing surf, but a moment later he'd be in danger again. My heart was racing just watching him.

But it wasn't just fear I was feeling. I was excited, probably almost as excited as Steve was. Watching him out there was incredibly thrilling. Steve was testing himself, pushing himself to the limit. He was doing something dangerous and daring. He was challenging the sea—and he was winning! I never wanted him to stop!

Suddenly, a bolt of lightning zigzagged across the sky, followed by a deafening crash of thunder. Almost immediately, it started to pour. Sick with fear, I jumped up and down, waving my arms and shouting, ''Steve! Come in! Come in!''

I saw Steve look up into the thick black clouds. Then he paddled for shore, using the powerful waves to push him in faster. Gasping for breath, he grabbed his surfboard and ran the last few yards to the beach.

Another bolt of lightning shot out of the clouds. ''Let's go!'' yelled Steve. He grabbed my hand and we ran for the car, barely noticing the heavy rain that cut into our faces. Steve threw his surfboard in the trunk and quickly tied the hood. Still panting, we jumped in the car and slammed the doors.

For a moment, neither of us spoke. Then I heard Steve whisper, but the rain splashed against the windshield, drowning out his words. I turned to face him. ''What did you say?''

Slowly, Steve's handsome face broke into a grin and with a whoop of joy, he thumped his hand against the steering wheel. ''I did it!'' he shouted triumphantly. ''I actually went out there and rode those waves!''

"Yeah," I agreed, grinning along with him. "Yeah, you did!''

We both threw back our heads and laughed with delight, oblivious to the rain, the cold, and the thunder that boomed all around us.

Chapter Thirteen

All the way home, Steve kept talking about what he'd done. He couldn't wait to drive over to Mark and T.J.'s and tell them he had surfed on those enormous waves. He was so excited, he hardly looked at the road. Fortunately, it didn't matter much. It was raining so hard there wasn't another car in sight, let alone a pedestrian.

While Steve talked, I nodded and smiled, but I wasn't really listening. Now that the initial thrill had worn off, I felt numb. Numb and a little shocked. I just couldn't believe Steve had actually gone out in that dangerous surf, right before a storm. It was just luck that had kept him from being drowned or electrocuted by a bolt of lightning.

For the first time since I'd met him, I found myself questioning Steve's judgment. Until then, his sense of adventure had been one of the things I liked best about him. He was brave, he was daring, he was going to surf on the most remote and exotic beaches in the world. But where did bravery end and stupidity begin? I wasn't sure, but right now it seemed to me that Steve possessed a fair share of both.

Before I could go any further with that line of thought, Steve turned on to West Avenue and I noticed that there were two cars in the Bensons' driveway. One was the Bensons' station wagon. No doubt they had hurried home after their brunch date in order to avoid the heavy rains. But who owned the second car? The windows of Steve's Mustang were so fogged up, I couldn't see well enough to tell.

It wasn't until we pulled up in front of the house that I recognized the second car. It was Chris's old gray Buick! "Oh, no!" I gasped.

"What's wrong?" asked Steve, turning toward me.

I struggled to keep the look of panic off my face. My heart was racing and my brain was going in twenty different directions at once. "Nothing!" I almost shouted. "I just remembered I left the oven on. I have to go!"

I struggled with the car door and finally pushed it open just as the Bensons' front door opened and Chris stepped onto the porch. "Hi, Kate!" he called, waving and smiling. "Surprise!"

Surprise? Heart attack was more like it! Chris hadn't told me he was coming to visit today. What in the world was he doing here? Immediately I began a silent prayer. Just let me disappear. I'll do anything. *Anything!*

But no such luck. Steve, naturally confused by my strange behavior, got out of the car. He still hadn't seen Chris. "Kate," he asked, "what's wrong?" Before I could answer, he walked over and put his arms around me. When I pulled away, he asked again, "What's wrong, Kate? Tell me."

At that moment, Steve looked up and saw Chris. Chris looked down at Steve. Neither boy said a word. And like an idiot, I just stood there, staring at my feet and feeling the rain drip down the back of my neck.

Chris walked over and put his arm possessively around my shoulders. "Who's this?" he asked suspiciously, tilting his head toward Steve.

"Steve Matheson," said Steve loudly, sticking his hand out toward Chris. "And who are you?"

"Chris Trower," answered Chris, shaking Steve's hand with false warmth. "Kate's boyfriend," he added, tightening his grip on my shoulders.

Just then the front door opened, and Bill looked out. "Hey, you kids. Get in here before you get soaked." He was smiling and holding the door open invitingly. There was nothing else to do but go in. Steve would have left, I suppose, but he followed us in, probably just to let Chris know he had a right to be there, too.

After we walked into the living room, Bill went off to get us some towels. Dee and Ricky immediately ran over to Steve and began showing him some new shells they'd found. It was obvious that they knew Steve well and liked him.

I glanced at Chris. I was pretty sure he could tell that Steve was more than just a casual friend of mine. Chris's arms were crossed tightly over his chest and he was staring at Steve with fire in his eyes.

Tina walked in from the kitchen and took in the whole scene quickly. "I'll make some tea," she said, throwing me a sympathetic glance as she left the room.

Bill soon returned with the towels. We all dried off and nervously sat down as far away from each other as possible. Bill left to join Tina in the kitchen and the kids followed, begging for cookies. I was left alone with Steve and Chris, who were sitting on the edge of their chairs, eyeing each other distrustfully.

What now? I racked my brain for something to say. "Well," I announced with a frozen grin, "it certainly is raining."

"Have you known Kate long?" asked Chris, never taking his eyes off Steve.

"All summer," he replied casually. "We surf together

every day. How about you?''

Chris looked as if he was about to explode. ''We've been going together for two years,'' he answered coldly.

Just then, Bill and Tina appeared with the tea. I'd never been so happy to see anyone in my life. I leaped up and tried to look busy helping Tina pour. Bill passed out cookies, which Chris and Steve refused, and the kids sat on the floor, stacking blocks and knocking them over.

When everyone had been given tea, we all sat down and sipped in uncomfortable silence. I noticed Bill looking at Steve, who was still wearing his bathing suit and wet-suit vest. ''Steve,'' he said, ''I hope you weren't planning to go surfing today.''

Steve didn't answer at first. I knew he wanted to boast about surfing in the storm, but he could tell that Bill would disapprove. ''Well, uh, I already . . .''

''Steve!'' exclaimed Tina. ''You didn't go out there, did you? Didn't you see the lightning? You could have been killed!''

''It was okay,'' I said quickly, trying to take the heat off Steve. ''It wasn't even raining when he went out, and I stood on the beach and watched for lightning.''

''What?'' cried Chris, leaping to his feet. Dee and Ricky stopped playing and stared at him. ''I can't believe you took Kate to the beach in this weather!'' Chris advanced toward Steve.

Now Steve stood up too. ''Look, I was the one who was surfing, not Kate. I wouldn't have let her even if she wanted to.''

''It's dangerous to go anywhere near the ocean during a storm,'' interjected Bill.

Chris glared at Steve and practically spit out the words, ''You fool! If Kate had been hurt, I-I—'' He was too angry to go on.

"Wait!" I cried, jumping up. "It was my fault. I—"

"I would *never* do anything to put Kate in danger," Steve said through clenched teeth. "Never!"

Slowly, Chris advanced toward Steve. Bill jumped up and put himself between them. "Now look here, you two—"

Steve laughed humorlessly. "Don't worry, Bill. I'm not going to hurt him. It would be much too easy." Steve turned on his heel and walked out the front door, letting the screen door slam behind him.

Before anyone could react, Chris turned to me. "Thanks a lot, Kate," he said sarcastically. "Thanks for not telling me you were dating someone else. It's much more fun being surprised."

For a second, I thought of lying to Chris. Maybe he would believe me if I told him Steve was just a friend. But it was much too late for that. The truth was long overdue. "I'm sorry, Chris," I said, as tears formed in my eyes. "I meant to tell you. I know it was wrong, but I . . ."

"Don't apologize," interrupted Chris. "I can understand how you fell for Steve. He's just your type—a big, dumb surfer."

I knew the Bensons were staring at us, but I didn't care. Chris had every right to be mad at me, but he had no right to criticize Steve. He was just being rude. "Chris Trower, how dare you!" I shouted. "Steve is more attractive, more intelligent, more athletic, more . . ."

Chris didn't wait to hear the rest. He walked quickly out the front door and slammed the screen, just as Steve had done. A few seconds later I heard the squeal of tires as his car took off up the street.

Miserably, I looked around the room. Dee and Ricky were sitting on the floor, looking frightened and confused. Bill was still standing beside me. He looked shocked and a little angry. Tina was still on the sofa, wearing an expression of sad concern. "Oh, Kate," she said softly, shaking her head.

That did it. I burst into tears and ran into my room. Flinging myself face down on the bed, I sobbed and sobbed. Everything was ruined. Everything. I had tried to keep two boyfriends and now I had none. My stupid lies had driven them both away.

I heard Tina walk into the room and whisper my name, but I didn't look up. How could I face her? Because of me, Chris and Steve almost had a fist fight in her living room. I kept crying and eventually I heard Tina close the door and walk away. Now I was alone, completely alone. I crushed my face into the pillow and sobbed. I'd never been so miserable in my life.

Chapter Fourteen

By the next day the rain had ended, but it was still windy and overcast. Considering my mood, the weather couldn't have been more perfect. I was miserable.

Most mornings, I slept soundly until Ricky roused me with his crying or his shouts of "Katie, wake up!" But today I woke up early and lay under the covers, reliving yesterday's horrible events over and over in my mind.

Hindsight is a wonderful thing. I now realized with total clarity that I should have broken up with Chris the moment I first met Steve. Chris is a great guy and he was a kind and loving boyfriend, but I knew now that I'd stopped loving him even before I left Fairbanks for the summer. It was only habit that had made me stay with Chris—that and the selfish fact that I enjoyed knowing how much he loved me.

I felt terrible about hurting Chris, but I wasn't sorry that we were no longer going steady. The thing that really upset me was losing Steve. At least, I was pretty sure I'd lost him. After meeting Chris, being criticized for taking me to the beach during the storm, and practically getting punched out in the Bensons' living room, I couldn't imagine him ever wanting to see me again.

The thought of never seeing Steve again brought fresh tears to my eyes. I didn't care if Steve was wrong to go surfing during yesterday's storm. I didn't care if he was wild, irresponsible, or just plain nuts. I loved his sky blue eyes, his silky blond hair and his easy laugh. I loved his sense of adventure and his passion for surfing. I loved the touch of his hands as he rubbed suntan lotion on my back and the feel of his lips as they brushed against mine. How could I go through life without him?

As I was asking myself that horrible question, Ricky woke up and called my name. Sighing deeply, I dragged myself out of bed and started my first day without Steve. Ricky seemed to have completely forgotten the fight he'd witnessed the night before, but Dee, who was older and wiser, asked, "Katie, who's your boyfriend now?"

"I don't know," I answered honestly, as we sat in the kitchen eating breakfast. "Probably no one." Dee looked sad as she picked at her scrambled eggs.

The kids and I spent the morning finger painting. Around eleven o'clock the sun broke through the clouds and I figured we could go outside after lunch. But before I could decide whether to open a can of tuna fish or stick with simple peanut butter and jelly, Tina appeared with a pizza and Cokes.

"I thought you might need cheering up," she said sympathetically.

"Thanks," I told her. "I do."

She sat down and opened the pizza box. "Has Steve called?" When I shook my head, she asked, "Why don't you call him?"

I frowned. I just couldn't call Steve. I was sure he never wanted to see me again. Besides, what would I say? "Maybe," I answered, just to please Tina. I didn't want her to keep talking about Steve because I was afraid I was going to cry.

"Listen, why don't you go surfing after lunch," suggested Tina. "I'll take care of the kids."

I didn't feel like doing much of anything, but I figured surfing would at least occupy my mind. I didn't want to appear irresponsible though, so I said, "I promised to take Dee surfing some afternoon. How about if I call Cindy and see if she can come with us?"

Ricky wanted to come too, but Tina appeased him with promises of a trip to the five-and-ten. I called Cindy and an hour later Dee and I met her at one of the quiet beaches at the northern end of the Island where there was almost no chance of meeting Steve.

While Dee eagerly waxed my board, I told Cindy what had happened yesterday. "Oh, wow, that's awful, Kate," she said. "Listen, do you want me to talk to Steve for you?"

"I don't know, Cindy. I don't think he wants to see me again. He was really mad when he left yesterday."

"Okay, but if you change your mind, just let me know. And why don't you stop by the bakery tonight? You can drown your troubles in chocolate chip cookies."

I laughed. "Okay, thanks." I turned to Dee, who was putting enough wax on my board to obscure the color. "Want to come out with me?" I asked her. "You can sit on my board."

"No," said Dee emphatically.

For some reason, Dee's stubborn refusal to go in the water suddenly made me mad. Probably I was just so preoccupied with my own problems that I didn't have any sympathy left for anyone else. "Don't be ridiculous, Dee," I said sternly. "The water won't hurt you."

"Yes, it will," she wailed, nervously eyeing the crashing surf.

"Oh, for goodness sake, grow up!" I grabbed my board and ran into the water, leaving Cindy to dry Dee's unhappy tears.

As soon as I paddled out, I regretted my angry words. Poor Dee! It wasn't her fault she'd fallen in the YMCA pool. To such a little girl, it must have been a really frightening experience. Promising to apologize to Dee as soon as I finished surfing, I turned my attention to the waves. I was so involved in practicing my turns that it was over an hour before I paddled in.

Cindy and Dee were making a sand castle. "Look, Kate!" said Dee, covering the towers with seaweed. She seemed to have forgotten that I'd yelled at her, but I apologized anyway. "I'm really sorry, Dee," I told her. "Can we kiss and make up?"

Dee planted a wet kiss on my cheek. "Hi, Steve," she said, smiling over my shoulder.

I turned around so fast, I put my knee in the middle of Dee's sand castle. Yes, it really was Steve, and he was walking right toward me. My heart skipped a beat as I gazed into his handsome face. And miracle of miracles, he was smiling!

"Hi, everybody," Steve said shyly. "Kate," he added, "can I talk to you a minute?"

"Come on, Dee," said Cindy. "I'll give you a ride in my boyfriend's pink jeep." Cindy hurried Dee away before she could change her mind.

Steve sat down beside me, but I suddenly felt too shy to look at him. I stared at my toes and waited uncomfortably for him to speak.

"I just came from your house," Steve said softly. "I apologized to Tina for dragging you along yesterday."

I looked up. "It wasn't your fault," I told him. "I came of my own free will. I was just as excited as you were."

Steve smiled. "I know. You're the only girl I've ever met who really loves surfing. That's one of the things I like about you." The smile disappeared. "Still, it was dangerous to go to the beach yesterday. No matter how great the waves were, it wasn't worth the risk. I knew that, but I went anyway and I let you come too. I'm really sorry, Kate. Can you forgive me?"

I looked at Steve in amazement. Did he really think he had to apologize to me? "I'm the one who should be apologizing," I said earnestly. "I never told you about Chris, and that was wrong. But Steve—" In my need to make him understand, I turned to him and put my hand on his arm. "I don't love Chris. I was just too lazy and too selfish to break up with him. It's you I love. Only you."

Fearfully, I removed my hand from Steve's arm and lowered my head. I was so afraid Steve was going to tell me he didn't love me. I pushed my toes in the sand and fought to hold back the tears.

"Little kitten." Steve put his fingers under my chin and lifted my head. His beautiful blue eyes were looking into mine. "It's hard to break up with someone," Steve said softly, "even if you know it's what you want. But all that's over with now. We're together and that's what counts."

Steve gently wiped a tear from my cheek and kissed me. "Surfer girl," he whispered, "I love you." I threw my arms around him and hugged him tight.

"Steve," I asked finally, "how did you know I was here?"

"I didn't. I just looked on every beach from one end of the Island to the other until I found you. Unfortunately, I started at the other end."

I laughed. "Well, I'm glad you kept looking."

"Me too," said Steve, "especially since there're only three weeks until the Championships. We've got to keep practicing." He jumped up. "Wait here while I get my board."

Steve went to the car and I turned to watch as he ran gracefully up the beach. It was hard to believe that only minutes ago I'd been totally miserable. Now that I knew Steve loved me, everything seemed fine. Happily, I whispered the words, "I love him." A shiver of delight slid down my spine as I added, "And he loves me too."

Chapter Fifteen

The next time I wrote to my parents, I told them all about Steve. I also explained that I had broken up with Chris, but I didn't go into the gory details. I guess I was embarrassed to let them know how poorly I'd handled the whole thing.

A few days later my parents called from the Poconos. "We've rented a little cabin out here in the woods for the weekend," my father told me. "It's right on a lake. Lots of canoeing and sailing. And Kate, I've done something surprising."

"What?" I asked eagerly.

"Oh, it's nothing big," he replied mysteriously. "You'll just have to wait until you see me."

Before I could question him further, my mother got on. "Katie, we got your letter. Are you sure you're doing the right thing?"

"Yes, Mom. Absolutely."

"Chris is such a nice boy," she went on. "I really thought you two cared for each other."

"We did, Mom, but a lot of things have changed." I thought about Chris's sensible goals—a basketball scholarship to Penn followed by law school and a good job. All that had sounded fine—or at least okay—until Steve came along. Now I knew life held other possibilities, other goals. Sure, I still wanted to go to college. But I wanted to surf too, and travel, and maybe even go to California with Steve.

I quickly realized I had a lot of things to talk to my parents about, but I figured I'd better wait until I saw them in person. Long distance is expensive! "You'll like Steve," I assured my mother. "He's so wonderful."

She laughed warmly. "If you like him, I'm sure he is."

"And wait until you see him surf. . . ."

"Oh, Kate. I almost forgot. Daddy and I thought we might come back to the Poconos instead of taking our vacation in Beach Haven this year. It's so lovely here."

"But Mom," I cried, "you have to come down for the Long Beach Island Championships. *I'm* surfing too!"

"What?" gasped my mother. I couldn't tell if it was a gasp of delight or horror. There was a pause and then she said uncertainly, "You entered a surfing contest?"

"Yes. It's the last Saturday in August. Can't you come?"

Mom put her hand over the receiver and conferred with Dad. "Of course we'll come," she said finally. "We'll just leave the Poconos a little early and drive down to Beach Haven the weekend of the contest." She paused and I waited uncomfortably, sure she was going to give me a lecture on the dangers of surfing. "And, Katydid," she said, "are you getting enough sleep?"

"Oh Mother!" I moaned, secretly relieved that the conversation was back to normal. "Of course I am!"

The rest of August practically flew by as Steve and I began seriously training for the Championships. Training

meant eating lots of good food (no more doughnuts from
the Bay Village Bakery), getting lots of sleep (no more
late nights at The Club), jogging, and surfing every day.
Except for the surfing, it wasn't exactly my idea of fun,
but I didn't complain. As long as I was with Steve, even
jogging across blistering sand under the hot August sun
seemed like a dream come true.

Steve still talked about going to California in September, but I didn't take him too seriously. His cousin in
Huntington Beach had lined up a job for him in one of the
local surf shops, but Steve's parents were still against the
idea. I tried to cheer Steve up by reminding him he could
stay in New Jersey and still go professional. He didn't like
the idea, but at least he admitted it was a possibility.

Then, as the last Saturday in August loomed closer,
Steve stopped talking about California and concentrated
completely on the Championships. The contest would be
held at a beach in Holgate, on the southern end of the
Island. We surfed there exclusively to get a feel for
the beach and the wave patterns. Steve also checked
out the final entry list to see who our competition would
be. There were lots of unknowns as well as a few highly
respected surfers coming up from Florida, but so far, I was
the only female. Since there was no women's division in
the Championships, that meant I would be the only girl
competing against thirty-five guys!

"Oh, Steve!" I cried when he told me. "I thought
there'd be at least a few other girls. What am I going to do?
I can't compete against all those guys!"

"Sure you can," replied Steve. "Just wear your black
bikini and you'll be sure to take a first."

"Steve!" I laughed and threw a towel at his head. "Be
serious!"

Steve tossed the towel back in my lap. "Okay, seriously," he said. "You're a better surfer than most of the guys on this Island, and I guarantee you're going to be better than most of the surfers who enter the Championships too." He put his hand on my shoulder and squeezed it gently. "Believe me, Kate, you're going to do just fine."

When Steve talked like that, I could believe *anything*. From then on, I put the other competitors out of my mind and just concentrated on my surfing. It seemed to work too. I was getting better all the time.

Although my days were filled with work, surfing and Steve, at night my thoughts still turned to Chris. I hadn't heard from him at all since the afternoon he walked out of the Bensons' living room, and I could just imagine how hurt and angry he must be. I wanted to call him, or at least write him a letter, but I just didn't know what to say. Somehow, "I'm sorry" seemed so inadequate, especially when I couldn't follow it with "I love you."

I knew I didn't love Chris anymore. Still, I couldn't help remembering all the good times we'd had together and all the plans we'd made for college and beyond. Why couldn't love end without everyone feeling so sad, I wondered.

Then around the middle of August I got a letter from Rachel. She told me about her job at McDonald's (she hadn't dropped any more hamburgers and she was dating the night manager) and about the new clothes she was planning to buy for school. After her signature, Rachel had added, "P.S. What's happening between you and Chris? I heard he's dating Linda Carson and I saw them together at the mall. Shawn Faber told me you're seeing someone at the shore. Is it true? Tell all!"

"It's true!" I wrote back. "His name is Steve and he's a surfer!" My letter was filled with praise for Steve and descriptions of the exciting things we'd done together. Writing about Steve made me happy, but as I sealed the envelope there were tears in my eyes. Suddenly, I missed Chris. I knew it didn't make sense, but I couldn't help it. It hurt to think of him with Linda Carson. He was probably taking her out to all the places he'd taken me, telling her all the same jokes, maybe even driving her to our special spot at Bowman's Cliff.

Now I know how Chris must have felt when he learned about Steve and me. But at least Chris didn't have to see me with Steve every day, the way I was going to see Chris and Linda around school.

My only consolation was knowing that Steve would be in New Jersey next year. We'd see each other every weekend and he could come up to Fairbanks for dances and football games. Maybe we'd even go on a surfing trip to Virginia Beach or Florida. With that thought in mind, I walked to the corner mailbox and determinedly dropped Rachel's letter in the slot.

The only time I wasn't surfing or thinking about surfing was the time I spent taking care of Dee and Ricky. We'd grown extremely close over the summer, so close that they sometimes called me Mommy Kate. I was the only one allowed to hold Dee's magic shell and the only one who could talk to Ricky's imaginary friend, Claude.

Still, I hadn't been able to cure Dee of her fear of water. She would play near the ocean and even wet her toes if I held her hand, but she wouldn't actually go in. Nothing—not my reassurances, my surfing, or even my anger—had helped.

Then one Saturday we were at the beach near the library, biding our time until the children's movies began at ten. Ricky was throwing lumps of sand into the water and Dee was playing catch with another little girl, when I saw an ice cream truck drive into the parking lot. As soon as the kids heard the bell, they began begging for ice cream, and since it was over two hours until lunch time, I agreed.

Leaving Dee to keep an eye on Ricky, I trudged up the beach to buy Fudgsicles. I was hurrying back with the ice cream melting down my wrists when I heard Ricky's frightened voice. ''Katie! Mommy Katie!''

I froze and scanned the beach for Ricky. I quickly spotted him, struggling in water well over his head. He must have waded out too far and been knocked over by a crashing wave. Instantly, I dropped the Fudgsicles and took off down the beach toward him.

But as I ran, I saw Dee running too. She was only a few feet from the water and she splashed into it without hesitation. She was in up to her shoulders before I could get halfway down the beach. By the time I reached the water's edge, she had caught Ricky in a bear hug and was dragging him onto the sand.

With a cry of joy and relief, I fell to my knees and threw my arms around both of them. Ricky was scared and crying, but otherwise fine. I looked at Dee. She seemed confused and frightened and I don't think she really understood what she'd done.

I smiled at her and said, ''Dee, you saved him.'' She looked up and smiled uncertainly. ''I'm so proud of you. You jumped right in and got Ricky. You're a hero!''

Ricky stopped crying to listen. ''Let's go home and tell Mommy and Daddy,'' I said. ''Let's go tell them how brave you are.''

''I'm brave too,'' said Ricky, not wanting to be left out.

''Yes, of course you are,'' I told him. ''You were in

that deep water and you knew to call for help. That was very brave and very smart.''

A group of people had gathered around us. ''Is he all right?'' asked a woman.

''Yes,'' piped up Dee. ''I saved him!'' She looked very pleased with herself.

As the crowd dispersed, I scooped up Dee and Ricky and started carrying them up the beach. ''Come on, little heroes,'' I said happily. ''Let's go home and celebrate!''

Chapter Sixteen

On the morning of the Long Beach Island Championships, I was up at 5 AM. Steve picked me up at 5:30 and we drove onto the mainland for a breakfast of steak and eggs at Rocky's All-Night Diner. By 6:30 we were on the beach, studying the waves along with three or four other early risers.

Sitting there shivering on the sand, everything seemed a little unreal. I could hardly believe the first heat of the Championships would be starting in a little over an hour, and I certainly couldn't believe I'd be competing. I looked at Steve. He was wearing his white trunks and a sleeveless T-shirt that said THE CURL: NEW JERSEY'S FINEST SURF SHOP. His new board—the one he had longed for ever since his trip to Virginia Beach—also bore an advertisement for The Curl.

Steve was staring at the waves and nodding. "Long and smooth," he said. "Just perfect." He turned to me. "Okay, Kate, now remember what we talked about. You can really rack up points on these waves if you can just stay on."

I nodded. We'd gone over this at least a dozen times already. The Championships would consist of seven pre-

liminary heats with five surfers each. Each ride was
scored by the judges and given points for wave size,
length of ride and surfing ability. When the points were
added up, the top twelve surfers would go on to the finals.
At the end of the day, the surfer with the most points
would win.

As Steve and I studied the waves, more surfers appeared. A group of workmen arrived and began setting up
the judges' table, loudspeakers, and a scoreboard. Ban-
ners were raised that proclaimed this to be the Third
Annual Long Beach Island Surfing Championships, spon-
sored by the Chamber of Commerce and the Southern
New Jersey Surfing Association.

Photographers and reporters arrived and crowded
around the well-known surfers, including Steve, who was
considered the most promising local. No one talked to me
or took my picture. I don't think they even realized I was
competing. That was just fine with me. All this activity
was making things a lot less unreal, and I was getting more
and more nervous by the minute. I walked away from the
crowd and started waxing my board slowly and methodically. I took deep breaths and tried to stay calm.

By eight o'clock the beach was crawling with people.
Cindy and Jeep stopped by to wish me luck before moving
to the spectators' area beside the judges' table. They were
dressed alike in leopard-print shorts, sunglasses, and
T-shirts that read THE SPIKES: BRAIN-BRUISING
ROCK AND ROLL. Bill and Tina stopped by too, carrying Dee and Ricky on their shoulders. Ricky was talking a
mile a minute, but Dee just stared at everything in fascinated silence. My parents still hadn't shown up.

Soon after eight the judges handed out our numbers
which Steve and I pinned to the backs of our T-shirts. The
surfers who would compete in each heat had been chosen

at random and while the judges wrote their names and numbers on the blackboard, I covered my arms and legs with suntan lotion. At this point, Steve and I both had our noses covered with Noxzema, as did many of the other surfers on the beach.

I was watching the judges write my name under Heat Number Five, when I felt someone tap my shoulder. I turned around to find a man grinning at me. He had short hair and a full beard peppered with curly streaks of gray. For an instant I was baffled, and then the shock of recognition made my mouth fall open. The man was my father. He had grown a beard!

As I stood staring in amazement, Dad hugged me and asked, ''Well, what do you think?''

I stepped back and laughed. ''You look like a beachcomber,'' I said. ''Or a surfer!''

''I thought I'd trim it a bit, but your mother seems to like it,'' he told me. ''Even the folks at work were impressed. What about you?''

My father looked a lot younger, almost like one of my brother's friends from college. It was strange to think of him that way, but I had to admit he looked pretty good. ''I like it,'' I said. ''You're cute.''

''I agree,'' said my mother, walking up behind Dad. She took a deep breath and began, ''Now, Kate, don't do anything dangerous out there. If you. . . .''

''There's Steve,'' I said, distracting my mother by pointing him out. He was being photographed with his surfboard. ''Isn't he fabulous?''

Before my parents could reply, a voice over the loudspeaker announced, ''Welcome to the Third Annual Long Beach Island Surfing Championships. All those not competing please return to the spectators' area. Surfers competing in the first heat should get ready to paddle out.''

My parents wished me luck, kissed me, and hurried away to the spectators' area. I checked the blackboard. Steve was in the first heat. I rushed down to the water to kiss him before he had to paddle out. He kissed me hurriedly, but I could tell his attention was completely focused on the crashing surf.

I walked back up the beach and sat down with the other surfers to watch. One of the judges waved a flag and the first five surfers, including Steve, threw their boards in the water and paddled out. Three of the surfers, I noticed, took off on the first wave they could catch. Steve and another boy, Number 18, waited for better waves and then took off. It soon became clear that only Steve and Number 18 were any good. Steve easily outrode the competition though, executing off-the-lips, fast turns and some amazing 360 degree maneuvers.

At the end of the heat, Steve joined me on the beach. It was typical of Steve that he wasn't completely satisfied with his performance, but when the judges posted the results, he had won his heat by twenty points.

Steve glanced at the names of the surfers in my heat, but the only one he knew was T.J. I didn't look forward to competing against one of Steve's best friends, but I couldn't help being a little pleased. I knew I was a better surfer than T.J.

By the time the fifth heat rolled around, I was a nervous wreck. Steve gave me a kiss and whispered, "Calm down. Just think about what you're doing and stay on as long as you can." I barely glanced at my competition, but I knew that except for T.J. they were all looking at me. After all, I was the only girl in the Championships. I'm sure they figured I'd be easy to beat.

By the time we paddled out, a group of photographers had gathered at the water's edge and were aiming their cameras at me. I tried to ignore them, but I was so nervous, I wiped out on my first ride. Slowly, I retrieved my board and got back on. I felt just terrible. What had ever made me think I could compete in the Championships? I was just a beginner. I wanted to paddle into the middle of the ocean and disappear.

Then I heard someone laugh. It was one of the other surfers, a tall, skinny guy with a lopsided smile. Angrily, I paddled back out. How dare he laugh at me? I felt my determination return. I was a good surfer and I was going to prove it. I waited for the next decent wave, took off and went through every trick I knew, riding the wave almost to the shore line.

After that, no one laughed, and I got three more good rides before the judges waved us in. I'd been so focused on my own surfing that except for the guy who laughed at me, I'd barely noticed my competitors. ''Those other guys were nothing,'' Steve told me. ''You practically blew them out of the water.'' When the results were posted, I'd won enough points to place 10th in the overall listings.

Overjoyed, I followed Steve to the dunes, where we anxiously watched the last two heats. At the end of the morning, Steve was first by fifteen points and I had placed 12th—just five points above my closest competitor. I could hardly believe it! I had made it to the finals!

''Steve!'' I shrieked. ''I made it!''

''Of course,'' he replied casually. ''You've got a terrific coach.''

Lunch was a couple of hot dogs bought from a vendor's truck and eaten with Steve, my parents, Cindy and Jeep. The conversation centered completely on surfing and Steve barely took his eyes off the water the whole time. I knew he was studying the waves which were subtly changing as the tide came in.

After lunch, I sat with all the finalists and waxed my

board. A few photographers took my picture, but most of
the reporters talked to Steve and a couple of finalists from
Florida. I was getting nervous again, but not as nervous as
I'd been before. I'd proved myself a competent surfer by
placing in the top twelve, and that was all I'd really hoped
for. I didn't expect to do well in the finals. I was more
concerned about Steve, who had a good chance of taking
first place.

"See that guy there," said Steve, indicating a husky
boy with black hair. "That's Billy McDonald. He beat me
in the East Coast Surf Classic. And that kid over there is
Corky Windham. He's been competing in California re-
cently."

As Steve went on, I realized I was surrounded by a
group of really tough competitors. These guys were serious year-round surfers, not beginners like me. As Steve
would say, they would probably blow me out of the water.

Before I could think too much about that, one of the
judges came over and lined us up along the shore. When
he waved his flag, all twelve of us paddled out. The water
was so crowded that half the battle was getting possession
of a good wave. Usually, I liked to hang back and wait for
an empty wave, but I couldn't do that now. I had to vie for
position with everyone else and do the best I could on any
wave I could get. As a result, my surfing was less than
thrilling.

Most of the time I was so busy surfing, I didn't have
time to look at the other surfers. I didn't even notice Steve.
Then finally, as I sat straddling my board, waiting for the
next wave, I heard his voice.

"Kate!" Steve was paddling out to join me. "You're
doing great," he told me. It was hard to believe Steve had
had time to watch me, but I gratefully accepted the com-
pliment.

Just then, a new set of waves appeared on the horizon.

"Let it go," Steve cautioned, as the first wave swelled beneath us. Other surfers were taking off, but we sat and waited as three more waves went by.

The next wave was perfect, better than anything we'd seen all day, and Steve started paddling. "Come on!" he yelled, and I followed, but as I took off, Steve pulled back, leaving me alone on the day's most incredible wave.

I couldn't believe it! Steve had given me his wave! My first impulse was to jump off, but that would have been ridiculous. Steve couldn't catch the wave now and he would never forgive me if I let it go to waste. With new determination, I let loose and did every maneuver I could think of, including a tube ride that was better than anything I'd ever pulled off before.

That was the last wave I caught before the heat ended and it was the one that made all the difference. When the results were posted, Steve had taken first place, Corky Windham was second and Billy McDonald was third. And I had placed sixth—better than I'd ever imagined possible!

Weak with exhaustion and joy, I hugged Steve and rested my head against his warm chest. But before I could even say anything, we were surrounded by people, laughing, shouting and patting us on the back. Steve was hustled off to accept his trophy and I stood with my parents and friends, grinning foolishly while they congratulated me and kissed me.

When Steve returned with his trophy, he was followed by photographers and reporters. The were from local papers, regional surfing newspapers, and even a national surfing magazine. They seemed as interested in me as they were in Steve and when Steve announced I was his girlfriend, they fell all over themselves to get pictures of the two of us together.

"What are your plans for the future?" asked one journalist.

"I plan to compete in California and Hawaii," answered Steve. "And eventually I hope to turn pro."

"How about you, young lady?"

"I just want to keep competing," I told them. "And then join Steve on the West Coast."

I caught a glimpse of my mother near the back of the crowd. She looked horrified, or maybe it was just surprise. I guess I was a little surprised myself. I'd never thought I would want to enter more surfing contests, but then I never thought I'd place in the top ten on my first try either. But thanks to Steve, I had done it. And as long as Steve was by my side, I knew I could do it again.

Chapter Seventeen

That night there was a big celebration at The Club. Everyone was there—not just the usual Long Beach Island crowd, but also surfers from out-of-town who had come to the Island to compete in the Championships. The Spikes were at their best, pounding out set after set of fast-paced dance songs, and the crowd was responding by dancing, clapping and singing along. Cindy sat in her usual spot at the edge of the stage, cheering on Jeep and the rest of The Spikes.

Steve and I spent the evening dancing and talking to everybody. I met dozens of surfers, including Corky Windham and Billy McDonald, the boys who had placed second and third behind Steve. All the surfers seemed very interested in me, and all the girls were fascinated by Steve. We were both enjoying the attention, but it was obvious to everyone that Steve and I were only interested in each other. We spent the whole evening side by side, either dancing or holding hands.

By midnight, I was exhausted and although I was having fun, I was relieved when Steve finally suggested we should leave. Outside The Club, he put his arm around my shoulders and said, "Let's walk on the beach. I have something important to tell you."

As we strolled beneath the streetlights, I tried to guess what Steve had to say. In only five days the Bensons would be returning to Fairbanks and I'd be going with them. I was looking forward to being home with my family and I was excited about seeing my friends again. But leaving the shore meant leaving Steve, and that was almost too horrible to think about.

How could I live without surfing and Steve? Once again I reminded myself that Steve would still be in New Jersey, less than two hours from Fairbanks. Maybe that was what he wanted to talk to me about. Maybe he wanted to reassure me that we'd still be able to see each other. We'd still be in love.

As we walked down the beach, Steve was trying without much success to suppress a smile. He looked excited and pleased. Now I was really curious. By the time we reached the water's edge, I couldn't stand it any longer. "What is it?" I demanded. "The suspense is killing me."

Steve's face broke into a delighted grin. He put his hands on my shoulders, looked me straight in the eye and said, "I'm going to California next month!"

"W-what?" A wave of sickness swept over me and settled in the pit of my stomach. My legs felt like seaweed and I grabbed Steve's waist to steady myself.

Steve thought I was hugging him. He held me close and said, "Isn't it great? I can hardly believe it myself!"

"But your parents," I managed. "The marina . . ."

"I know. Up until last night my dad was still saying no, and I'd just about decided I was going to California anyway, even if it meant never seeing my parents again."

Steve stepped back and looked at the waves as they crashed methodically against the sand. I tried to smile so

Steve wouldn't notice the tears in my eyes. "So what happened?" I asked.

"My father and I had a huge fight. It wasn't much fun at the time, but in retrospect I can see it was the best thing that could have happened. It really cleared the air. I told my dad I was going to California with or without his permission. At first he was furious, but after a while we both settled down and started talking."

"That's great," I said, trying to feel pleased.

"Yeah. We really got down to feelings. I think we understand each other a lot better now. And we made a deal. I'm going to live with my cousin and work at the surf shop in Huntington Beach, just like I wanted. In return, I promised my dad I'd go to college part-time. I'm going to look into it when I get out there and enroll for the spring semester."

Steve sat on the sand and I dropped down beside him. "Well, what do you think?" he asked.

What could I say? Steve had a faraway look in his eyes and I knew he was thinking about California. In his mind he was already there, making new friends, surfing new beaches and finding a new girl to love. Even though Steve still sat beside me, his arm draped carelessly around my shoulders, I knew I had already been left behind. In a few weeks he'd be leaving for California. He didn't have time for me.

I took a deep breath to hold back the tears. "That's wonderful," I said. "Just great."

But Steve was barely listening. "Let's walk," he said, jumping to his feet. "I'm so excited, I can't sit still."

As we walked along the beach, Steve talked about California. He told me about his cousin Nick and all the things Nick had written to him about Huntington Beach.

He talked about the West Coast surfing contests that would be coming up in the fall and which ones he planned to enter. He reminisced about the Long Beach Island Championships and said that winning had made him feel even more certain that going to California was the right thing. He even talked about the clothes he planned to take and what surfboards were best for West Coast surfing.

Through it all, I smiled and nodded. After all, I told myself, why shouldn't Steve go to California? It was what he'd always wanted, what he'd planned all along. He never made any secret about it, so there was no reason for me to be surprised.

But what about me? I wanted to scream. What about our summer together—the surfing, the dancing, the conversations and the kisses? Didn't they count for anything? And what about our dream of surfing around the world together? Hadn't Steve been serious about that? Had it all been a joke?

Then I thought about Chris. Sweet Chris—so kind, so loving, so devoted. I remembered the night of the sports banquet and the argument we'd had in the parking lot of Jimmy's Steak House. Chris had practically begged me to spend the summer in Fairbanks with him, but I'd refused to listen. "I guess you figure you'll meet some handsome surfer this summer," Chris had told me.

Chris's words echoed inside my head as I turned to look at Steve. He was still walking beside me, smiling and laughing as he talked on and on about California.

Well, Chris, I thought sadly, you were right. I *did* meet a handsome surfer this summer. The only problem is, he left and broke my heart.

I moved through the next few days like a sleepwalker.

My parents stayed at the shore until Sunday afternoon, but I told them Steve couldn't meet us for lunch because he had to visit his grandparents. I couldn't bear to tell them he didn't love me anymore, especially after my mother had questioned my decision to break up with Chris.

After my parents left, the days dragged on monotonously. Every morning I took care of Dee and Ricky and every afternoon I sat alone in my room. Steve didn't call or come to see me. He was probably surfing every afternoon, but I didn't go to the beach to find out. At night I hung around the Bay Village Bakery, eating too many cookies while Cindy tried to cheer me up.

Sometimes I felt mad at Steve, but mostly I just felt sad. After all, we hadn't made any promises. It was just a summer romance and now it was over. That's what I told myself, but I still felt terrible. And whenever I remembered how happy Steve had looked when he told me about California, my eyes filled with tears.

The Bensons and I were leaving Beach Haven on Friday. That meant Thursday afternoon would be my last chance to go surfing until next summer. Even though surfing reminded me of Steve, I still loved the thrill of riding down the face of a smooth green wave, and I wanted to do it one more time before I went home.

On Thursday afternoon, Bill dropped me off in Holgate and I carried my board to the beach. I picked a quiet beach, one that Steve rarely surfed, and paddled out. The waves were small but smooth, just the way I like them. I threw myself into the act of surfing so completely that for the first time in days, I was able to forget about Steve. It was as if my mind had been turned off and only my body was in control. I cut across the slippery waves with total abandon and for the first time all week, I felt good.

When I was too exhausted to paddle anymore, I lay on my board and let the waves carry me in. Struggling to shore, I threw down my surfboard and flopped on the sand, oblivious to everything except the warm sun on my back.

"Kate!"

With a gasp, I rolled over. Steve was standing there looking down at me with his hands on his hips and a shy smile on his face. "W-what are you doing here?" I sputtered foolishly.

"Tina told me you were here." Steve knelt down and ran his hand over my cheek. "I'm sorry I scared you, little kitten. I'm just so happy to see you."

I wanted to answer, but instead I burst into tears. Steve slipped his arms around me and held me close. "Kate," he whispered. "Don't cry. Tell me what's wrong."

"What's wrong?" I repeated incredulously, pulling away and staring at him. I was so angry I stopped crying. "First you tell me you're leaving for California. Then you don't even call or come see me. Don't you care about leaving me? Don't you even want to say good-bye?"

"Kate, oh Kate." Steve shook his head and sighed deeply. "Of course I care about leaving you. I care so much, I don't know what to do. That's why I haven't seen you since Saturday night. I've been sitting in my room, thinking about you and trying to figure out a way to be in two places at once." He laughed ruefully. "Don't you see? I want to go to California and I want to stay here with you too."

"But why didn't you say that Saturday night?" I asked tearfully. "You sounded so happy then."

"I *was* happy. I was happy that my parents had finally given in and I was excited about going to California—so excited that I couldn't think of anything else. Then when I told you, you seemed pleased, and I just got carried away, talking about my plans. It wasn't until the next day that I realized how much I was going to miss you.''

"Oh Steve," I whispered. "I love you."

Steve reached for my hand. "I love you too, Kate, more than I ever realized. I didn't think anyone or anything could change my mind about leaving New Jersey, but now I don't know if I can stand to go, at least not if it means losing you.''

I looked at Steve's sad blue eyes. At that moment, I think he was about ready to give up his plans and stay in New Jersey with me. All I had to do was ask. But suddenly I knew I couldn't. Steve is a good surfer, maybe even a great one, and for him, moving to the West Coast was a dream come true. I just couldn't ask him to give up his dream for me, not if I really loved him. I would have been selfish and unfair.

"Steve," I said with conviction. "You're going to California."

He frowned. "I want to, Kate. You know that. But I don't want to lose you."

"You won't," I promised. "I'll still love you whether you're in New Jersey, California, or halfway around the world."

"And will you write to me?"

I laughed. Ten minutes ago, I was sure Steve didn't love me, and now *I* was the one reassuring *him*. "Of course, silly."

Steve leaned over to kiss me, and his face was flushed with excitement. "Maybe you can come out for Christmas," he said. "I'd love to see you surf on those big West Coast waves."

"Who knows?" I answered. "Maybe after I graduate I can move out and join you."

Steve put his hands on my shoulders and looked at me with his beautiful sky blue eyes. "And someday we'll surf around the world together." He leaned over and kissed me. "Just me and my special surfer girl."

Chapter Eighteen

September 7th dawned sunny and bright, no different from any other morning that week. But for me it was a very special day, a day that marked both an end and a beginning. It was the first day of school—the beginning of my senior year—and it was the day Steve was leaving New Jersey for his new life in California.

At breakfast that morning, I picked at my scrambled eggs and thought about school. After such an incredible summer, it was hard to get excited about one more year at Fairbanks High. Sure, I was looking forward to seeing my friends, and I was interested in competing on the swim team. Other than that though, school didn't hold much interest for me.

For one thing, Steve wouldn't be around to share it with me. While I was doing calculus problems and reading Shakespeare, he would be in Huntington Beach, swimming, surfing and making new friends. My only consolation was that he promised to write, call every week and send lots of pictures. Meanwhile, I planned to start working on my parents, trying to convince them to let me visit Steve over Christmas vacation.

The other problem with school was Chris. I wasn't

looking forward to meeting up with him and I dreaded the thought of seeing him with Linda Carson. I still felt I owed him an apology but I didn't know quite what to say, or if he would even listen. All I could do was play it by ear, and hope he could somehow forgive me.

I was just about to leave for the bus stop when the phone rang. My mother answered it upstairs and then called, "Don't leave yet, Kate. It's for you."

Surprised, I picked up the downstairs phone and said, "Hello?"

"Hey, surfer girl, I miss you already!"

"Steve!" I gasped. "Where are you?"

"At the airport. My plane leaves in fifteen minutes."

I laughed with delight. "Well, don't miss it, silly. You wouldn't want to be late for those Huntington Beach waves."

"Don't worry," Steve assured me. "I'll be surfing on them this afternoon." He paused. "And Kate, I'll send you a shell from Huntington Beach. I want you to hold it to your ear and pretend I'm whispering 'I love you.' "

I sighed happily. "And pictures," I reminded him. "Be sure to send lots of pictures."

"Uh-oh," said Steve. "They're calling my plane. Good-bye, little kitten. I have to run. Have a good first day of school."

"Good-bye, Steve. Good-bye." I hung up and let the memory of Steve's voice fill my head. Dreamily, I glanced up at the clock.

Five after eight! Grabbing my books, I ran out the door and jumped on the school bus, just as it was pulling away from the curb.

The first day of school was ridiculously hectic. I was so busy listening to teachers and writing down homework assignments that I barely had time to miss Steve all morning. I managed to talk to Amy and Rachel between classes, and we promised to meet at the mall after school for sodas and conversation. I didn't see Cindy, or Chris and Linda Carson at all.

When the lunch bell rang, I hurried through the line and carried my tray into the cafeteria. Rachel and Amy, my usual lunch companions, were nowhere in sight, but I noticed a couple of girls I knew from the swim team. I was just about to head for their table when I saw Chris. He was walking in the door with Linda Carson and the two of them were holding hands.

I wanted to act nonchalant, but somehow I just couldn't. Chris had been my boyfriend for two years, and even after all that had happened, it still hurt to see him with another girl. Instead of sitting down, I stood there staring as my lunch tray grew heavy in my hands.

Should I sit down or should I talk to him? Luckily, Chris didn't see me so I didn't have to decide. He and Linda joined the lunch line while I stood there stupidly, wondering what to do next.

"Kate!" I looked around. "Hey, Kate, come on over!"

It was Cindy, sitting at a corner table with a group of her friends. Last year I thought they were all so weird looking, but after a whole summer of hanging around with Cindy and The Spikes, they seemed pretty normal. Even the girl with the blue hair looked okay.

Still, I was reluctant to go over to Cindy's table. Being friends on Long Beach Island was one thing, but Fairbanks High School is a whole different scene. The school is divided into cliques and there's very little socializing between them. Cindy's clique and mine were about as far apart as you could get. In fact, they actively disliked each other.

Before I could decide what to do, Cindy jumped up and came over. "I saw you looking at Chris," she said sympathetically. "Come on over and pig out on some chocolate chip cookies with me. I brought a whole pile of them home from the shore."

When Cindy said that, I felt ashamed that I'd even considered not sitting with her. It wasn't that I liked being stuck in a clique, it's just that until I met Cindy, I never knew how to break out of it. But now, I realized, I had a chance. Cindy and I were friends at the shore and there was no reason why we couldn't be friends at Fairbanks High School too. We just had to loosen up and do it.

I smiled gratefully. "Cindy, you're a real friend. Thanks."

"Any friend of The Spikes is a friend of mine." Cindy grinned and led me back to her table.

When the last bell rang, I grabbed my books and hurried out the door. I was supposed to meet Rachel and Amy at the mall in an hour. Usually I took the bus, but when I left the school and felt the warm sun hit my face, I decided to walk, even though the mall is over a mile away.

I was heading across the parking lot when I saw Chris getting into his old gray Buick. My first impulse was to run the other way, but I forced myself to keep walking. I couldn't go on avoiding Chris forever. If I was going to apologize, I had to do it now. Otherwise, I'd just fall back into my old pattern of ignoring anything that seemed unpleasant. I couldn't do that anymore.

"Chris!" I called before I could chicken out.

He turned quickly and when he saw me, his face looked

sad. "Hi, Kate," he said. "How are you?"

"Okay," I said and then paused. I didn't know what to say next.

"Can I give you a ride anywhere?" Chris opened the door on the driver's side.

"Well, I'm meeting Amy and Rachel at the mall. . . ."

"Hop in. I'll drive you over."

Apprehensively, I walked around the car and got in. Chris started the car and without a word we left the parking lot and turned into the street.

Sitting in Chris's car brought back a flood of memories. I remembered all the times we'd driven to Bowman's Cliff and sat side by side in the backseat, kissing and whispering together. I remembered the sad look on Chris's face as he sat in the car after our fight in the parking lot of Jimmy's Steak House. And I remembered hearing the squeal of Chris's tires as he backed out of the Bensons' driveway.

"Are you going to get a chance to go surfing this winter?" Chris asked.

"I might go out to California," I said. "If I can convince my parents."

"That would be great. Our family is going to Puerto Rico in February."

"Terrific." I turned to Chris. "Chris, I want to talk to you. I—"

But before I could say anymore, a car ran a red light and Chris had to swerve across the road to get out of the way.

"Idiot!" Chris yelled out the window. "We could have been killed."

The next thing I knew, we were pulling into the parking lot of the mall. Chris took a space and turned off the car. This was my last chance. I had to apologize now. I had to explain. "Chris," I began. "About this summer . . . I'm so sorry. I shouldn't have lied to you. I was—"

"No," said Chris. "You don't have to apologize." He looked at me and smiled. "I should have been less possessive and you should have been more honest. We both know that now."

"I know, Chris, but—"

"Listen, Kate. When I saw you with Steve, it really made me mad. It took me a long time to get over feeling hurt and betrayed." Chris paused. "But I did get over it, enough to realize that it wasn't anybody's fault. It was just time for us to break up, that's all."

I sighed. "I guess you're right. I just wish it hadn't hurt so much."

"Me too." Chris smiled. "But that was the summer, and this is now. It's going to be impossible to avoid each other all year, Kate. So what do you say we just agree to be friends? Okay?"

Impulsively, I leaned over and kissed Chris on the cheek. "Okay," I said. Before he could react, I jumped out and slammed the door. "Thanks for the ride!" I called.

Chris laughed. "Anytime!" He started his car and drove away.

As I watched Chris drive out of the parking lot, I realized I was smiling. I was just so glad I had finally gotten up the courage to talk to Chris. If I hadn't, we might have gone through the whole year avoiding each other and feeling bad. Now at least we could face each other without wanting to run away. And if we were really lucky—and if I could get over seeing Chris with Linda Carson—we might even learn to be friends.

When Chris's car was out of sight, I turned and walked into the mall. Lots of kids from my school were there, looking in stores or just hanging out. It felt good to be there with them and I realized I was actually starting to look forward to my senior year. The only hard part was going to be living without Steve, but now somehow I felt even that wasn't going to be so bad. After all, there would be letters and phone calls to look forward to, and the possibility of a whole lifetime together after that.

And even if things didn't work out, even if we never fulfilled our dream of surfing around the world together, we would always have last summer to remember. I thought of all the fun we'd had—surfing, dancing, walking on the beach, kissing under the moonlight. I remembered our nights at The Club, my friendship with Cindy, mornings with Dee and Ricky, and winning sixth place in the Long Beach Island Championships. It really had been an incredible summer.

''Kate! Hey, Kate!'' I looked up to see Rachel and Amy waving to me from the other side of the mall. Putting aside my daydreams—at least temporarily—I waved back and hurried to join my friends.

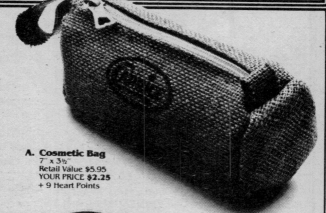

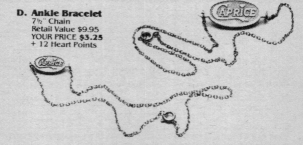

Now that you're reading the best in teen romance, why not make that *Caprice* feeling part of your own special look? Four great gifts to accent that "unique something" in you are all yours when you collect the proof-of-purchase from the back of any current *Caprice* romance!

Each proof-of-purchase is worth 3 Heart Points toward these items available <u>only</u> from *Caprice*. And what better way to make them yours than by reading the romances every teen is talking about! Start collecting today!

Proof-of-purchase is worth 3 Heart Points toward one of four exciting premiums bearing the distinctive *Caprice* logo

CAPRICE PREMIUMS
Berkley Publishing Group, Inc./Dept. LB
200 Madison Avenue, New York, NY 10016

PROOF OF
PURCHASE
—3—
HEART POINTS

DETAILS INSIDE

THE KEEPING DAYS SERIES—
Norma Johnston

☐ 29399-9	GLORY IN THE FLOWER	$2.50
☐ 43276-X	THE KEEPING DAYS	$2.50
☐ 54727-3	A MUSTARD SEED OF MAGIC	$2.50
☐ 16834-0	MYSELF AND I	$2.25
☐ 57434-3	A NICE GIRL LIKE YOU	$2.50
☐ 74954-4	THE SANCTUARY TREE	$2.50